SKIN DEEP

By

Pamela Clare

SKIN DEEP

Print Edition

Published by Pamela Anne Clare, 2012

Cover image and design by Jenn LeBlanc

Copyright © 2012 by Pamela Clare

ISBN-10: 0983875944

ISBN-13: 9780983875949

Hey, I-Team fans, this one is for you…

CHAPTER 1

Nathaniel West ignored the pain in his right arm and shoulder as he carried the case of frozen ground beef through the community kitchen's back door. He felt a tug of disappointment when he saw she wasn't there. Tall and willowy with creamy skin, bright green eyes, and thick auburn hair that hung in glossy waves down her back, she often volunteered in the kitchen in the afternoons.

Nate didn't know her name.

"Hey, man." Rev. Marshall hurried toward Nate. He looked more like a retired pro wrestler than a preacher, his clerical collar and flour-specked apron seeming at odds with his big, muscular body. "Thanks! I'll take that."

Nate handed over the case of beef. "How's it going, Reverend?"

"We're getting by, thanks to good folks like you." Rev. Marshall lugged the heavy box toward the walk-in freezer.

"Happy to help." Donating ground beef from the family's herd of black Angus cattle to community shelters and soup kitchens was a West family tradition.

Rev. Marshall disappeared inside the freezer, his voice calling back to Nate. "We're up to two hundred fifty for both lunch and supper, and it's growing. There's a lot of folks out of work these days. But with Thanksgiving coming, donations are picking up. The good Lord provides. Praise Jesus!"

The reverend's words set off a round of "amens" from volunteers, one of whom looked up, caught a glimpse of Nate's face, then looked quickly away, her smile now strained.

Nate turned and walked outside to the delivery truck, a cold wind whistling through the alley, carrying with it the mingled scents of car exhaust and snow. He opened the truck's back door, grabbed the next case of meat, carrying the remaining three boxes into the kitchen one at a time. He could've gotten a dolly and made a single trip—each case weighed exactly fifty pounds—but that would have defeated the purpose of making the delivery himself.

Though he was a good two years beyond the explosion that had nearly killed him, he was still far from the man he'd been, his right arm weak, the tendons in his elbow and shoulder stiff, his scarred muscles constricted. He needed to exercise his arm and chest as much as he could. And, although he didn't much care for coming into town, he had to get off the ranch once in a while and spend time with people other than his old man.

Or so his old man said.

It was getting easier—the stares, the whispers, the shock and revulsion on people's faces. The way people tried not to look, averting their gazes only to sneak a covert glance as he passed. The honest curiosity and fear of children, pointing and asking, "Mommy, what happened to that man's face?"

An IED—improvised explosive device—is what had happened.

He and the rest of his fourteen-man MSOT—Marine Special Operations Team—had been traveling with a four-man team of Navy SEALs on their way back from a joint mission in Afghanistan when their convoy was hit by an IED. One moment he'd been talking with Max about the sheer quantity of heroin produced in Kandahar Province and the next...

A pop. A hiss.

A deafening blast.

Blinding light. Searing pain.

Nate's helmet and combat goggles had protected his scalp, eyes and right ear, but the right side of his upper body, including his face, had been a mess of second- and third-degree burns. The surgeons had done what they could, saving his fingers, replacing charred flesh with skin grafts, giving him a new right nostril that almost looked real. But even after more than twenty surgeries, the right side of his face still looked like someone had painted his skin on with sloppy strokes of a putty knife.

Nate had been lucky.

Of the eighteen men in that convoy, three had been killed and six seriously maimed. Max had died instantly, blown to bits. Cruz had lost both legs AK—above the knee—along with his dick and right testicle. O'Malley's arms had been burned so badly that his fingers were gone, his hands misshapen stumps. Garcia had lost an eye and part of his brain to shrapnel.

As an officer, Nate had tried to focus on his men, encouraging them through phone calls and emails, holding it together for their sake. They were Marines. More than that, they were elite operators— the best the Marines had to offer. They would show the world what real strength and courage were by getting strong again and finding new ways to serve their country.

Only it hadn't been quite that simple.

The body recovered as best it could, but the spirit...

Cruz hadn't been able to face life without a real penis and had eaten a bullet. O'Malley had been hospitalized twice for prescription drug overdoses that Nate doubted were accidental. Garcia could barely talk and would never live independently again.

As for Nate, he wasn't a vain man, or he didn't think he was. As soon as the tubes had been taken out of his throat, he'd asked the nurses to bring him a mirror. While the nurse had held it, he'd stared himself right in the face, bandages off, and decided that he could live with what he saw.

Rachel hadn't felt the same.

She'd broken off their relationship with a tearful apology, unable even to look at him. "I can't do this, Nate. I can't do this."

She'd liked seeing him in uniform, but she'd never truly supported his decision to re-up. Still, her betrayal had hit him with the force of a second IED blast.

He'd put her out of his heart, out of his mind, doing his best to stay positive through months of agony—excruciating debriding treatments that had left him fighting not to scream despite high doses of morphine, repeated surgeries, incessant itching beneath pressure bandages. But the more he'd healed on the outside, the deader he'd become inside.

Post-traumatic stress, his therapist had said. Give yourself time, she'd said.

Yeah, well, no shit. It didn't take a PhD to figure that out.

Nate had come home to Colorado, hoping the mountain air and working with horses again would help him get his head on straight and regain strength in his arm, chest and shoulder. He *was* getting stronger. But inside, he was numb. He rarely left the ranch, and when it came to women—hell, he couldn't even begin to go there.

Nate had just handed the last case of beef over to Rev. Marshall, when the door from the dining area opened and *she* breezed in.

Her auburn hair was drawn back in a ponytail, her cheeks flushed from working at the steam table out front, an apron tied around her slender waist. "We're almost out of mashed potatoes. Sorry to run out on you, but I need to pick up Emily from preschool before six."

"You go get that sweet baby girl." Rev. Marshall disappeared into the freezer once again. "We'll see you next week."

"Good night!" a volunteer called.

"See you, Megan."

So her name was Megan.

She untied her apron, tossed it into a nearby laundry bin, then reached beneath the counter for her purse and jacket, her gaze meeting Nate's.

A strange awareness passed through him, like sunlight warming his skin.

She smiled, not a hint of revulsion on her pretty face as she slipped into her jacket and zipped it up to her chin. "Good night!"

Nate found his gaze following her as she hurried past him and out the back door.

Megan Hunter hurried across the street toward the parking lot, holding the collar of her jacket shut against the wind, the cold seeming to pass right through her. Teeth chattering, she took out her keys and double-clicked the button that unlocked the doors to her little blue Honda Civic. She'd no sooner sat in the driver's seat and shut her door, than he was there in the passenger seat beside her.

Donny.

Her heart gave a hard knock. "Wh-what are you doing here? Get out! Go before I call the police! If they find out you've violated the restraining order again—"

"Shut the hell up, Megan." Bony fingers closed around her wrist, preventing her from reaching into her purse for her cell phone. "I don't give a goddamn about the restraining order. I'm hurting for money, and I know you got plenty."

Donny had aged since she'd last seen him almost a year ago, his face haggard, his skin sallow, his teeth rotting in his mouth. He'd lost weight, too. Sweat beaded on his forehead, and there was an agitated glint in his eyes.

Meth.

She'd been scared before. Now she was terrified.

Not wanting to provoke him, she did her best to hide her fear. "H-hand me my purse. I'll give you everything I have."

As if seeing her handbag for the first time, he dumped its contents onto his lap and grabbed her wallet, searching through it, taking whatever cash she'd had. He shook the money in her face. "Twelve bucks? All you got is a lousy twelve bucks? Where's all the fucking money you got from the settlement?"

That's why he'd come after her. He'd read about the court settlement in the papers.

But Megan wasn't going to let him bully her. She wasn't the woman she'd been those years ago when she'd met him. She was stronger now, smarter. She had her life back, and she wasn't going to let him hurt her. "I don't have the money with—"

"Listen, bitch, you don't understand." He leaned forward and glared into her eyes, the stench of his breath overpowering. "I've fallen in with a rough crowd, and if I don't get them their money real soon, I'm in deep shit."

It was then Megan noticed the other car, the one that had pulled up behind her, blocking her. She was trapped. Chills slid down her spine that had nothing to do with the cold.

Oh, God! Oh, God! Oh, God!

"Here's what you're going to do. You're going to drive to the bank and withdraw five grand for me. Better make it ten. If you don't..." He plucked out a photo of Emily and threw it in Megan's face. "Cute kid."

Megan's blood turned to ice. "Y-you wouldn't hurt her."

"I might not, but those guys?" He pointed toward the other car with a jerk of his head.

"I-I'll go get your money and meet you back here."

Donny slapped her, the blow taking her by surprise, making her cheek burn. "You think I'm stupid? Me and you are going together. I'm not giving you a chance to call that asshole brother of yours or his cop frien—"

The passenger door opened and hands shot inside, grabbing Donny by the throat and dragging him backward out of the car. For one terrible moment, Megan feared the men in the other car had lost patience with her and were making a move. A scream welled up in her throat—then died when she recognized the scarred face of the man from the community kitchen.

He flung Donny aside, a look of fury contorting his damaged features, his expression softening when his gaze met Megan's. "Are you okay?"

She tried to warn him. "Y-yes, but the men in the other car—"

"Get down!" He dropped to one knee, a gun appearing in his hand.

Megan ducked down, covering her ears, unable to hold back a scream as gunshots split the icy air.

Bam! Bam! Bam!

Tires squealed. Another shot. *Bam!* A grunt.

"Damn it!" The man swore. "Shit! Well, they're gone."

She opened her eyes to see her rescuer rubbing his left shoulder with his scarred right hand, no sign of Donny or the other car. "Are you … Are you okay?"

The man nodded. "Yeah."

And then sheer panic kicked in.

"Emily!" Megan searched frantically on the floor of her car for her keys, which she must have dropped. "Oh, my God! Emily! They're going after get my little girl!"

"Call the cops. They'll get to her faster than you can, and they'll be able to protect her."

Something in his voice calmed the hammering of her heart, taking the sharpest edge off her fear. She looked up into dark blue eyes and took in his appearance all at once—short brown hair, dark eyebrows, strong jaw, firm mouth, high cheekbones. The right side of his face and neck were scarred from what could only have been burns, while the left was unhurt. But what struck her most was the concern in his eyes.

She nodded, retrieving her iPhone from the floor of the car.

But he had already pulled his cellphone out of his pocket and was dialing 911. "I want to report an assault and shots fired on Forty-sixth Avenue across from Denver Community Kitchen. The shooters fled the scene and headed south in a black Lincoln Continental with tinted windows. One assailant is on foot—white male, mid-to-late forties, about five-eleven and one-forty. He threatened the victim's child, so we think he may be on his way to the child's preschool located at… " He paused, looking to Megan.

"The man's name is Donny Lee Thomas." She also gave him the address and name of Emily's preschool, then dialed her brother's number, praying he would answer.

"Hey, Megan, what's—"

"Oh, Marc!" Choking back tears, she rushed to explain. "Donny tried to rob me. He jumped into my car—I think he was hopped up on meth—and he tried to steal money. He hit me. He's gone now, but he threatened to hurt Emily!"

"Son of a bitch!" Marc swore. "Where are you? Are you alone?"

"I'm across the street from the community kitchen, and no, I'm not alone. The man who fought Donny off me is still here, and he's armed. He's already called 911." Megan realized she didn't know the man's name. "Someone needs to go to the preschool and protect Emily."

Marc seemed to be speaking with someone else, then came back on the line. "Stay where you are, sweetheart. Dispatch has got two units headed your way. I'll get Emily. That bastard won't get near her."

She hung up, heard the sound of approaching sirens, her body starting to shake as relief set in. She looked over at the man who squatted down by her passenger side door. "Thank you."

He watched her, still on the phone with dispatch. "You're welcome."

"I've seen you at the kitchen. You're the rancher who donates all that ground beef."

He nodded, held out his hand. "Well, actually, I'm his son. The name's Nathaniel West."

"I-I'm Megan Hunter." She felt his fingers close around her trembling ones, and, surprisingly, she felt no desire to pull away like she usually did when a man touched her. In fact, she found the contact reassuring. "I can't thank you enough, Nathaniel."

Nate stood in the shadow of the community kitchen waiting for word that he was good to go. He'd already given his statement to the police. They'd asked him a thousand questions and confiscated his firearm, explaining that they would need the forensic evidence it would provide should they find the car he'd shot. They'd offered to call an ambulance to treat the graze on his shoulder, but he'd declined. It wasn't anything he couldn't handle himself.

"That's the second time you've been a blessing to us today, Mr. West." Rev. Marshall came up beside him and pressed a mug of coffee into his hand. "The Almighty was looking out for Megan this evening, that's for sure. That poor girl has been through enough, I mean to tell you."

Wondering what the reverend meant by that, Nate accepted the steaming mug and sipped.

"You're ex-military, aren't you?" Rev. Marshall seemed to study him.

Nate nodded. "Marines."

"That's right." The reverend nodded. "I remember your dad telling me something about that. You were wounded, burned bad. Looks like they fixed you up good as new though."

"Yeah." Right. Good as new.

Nate hoped the reverend would drop it.

"Seems like you've been through enough, too, but I'm mighty glad you were here. I thank you for your service on both accounts." The reverend stuck out his right hand.

"Thank you, sir." Nate accepted it, gave it a shake, strangely touched by the praise.

Truth was, what had happened tonight had gotten his heart beating in a way nothing had since the explosion. He'd felt blood pumping in his veins, rage surging through him when he'd seen that bastard strike her. It had felt *good* to act, to *do* something, to feel needed again.

He watched as Rev. Marshall walked back inside the kitchen, then looked across the street to where Megan sat in her car giving her statement to a uniformed police officer. Even at this distance, Nate could see she was crying. He found himself wishing he could have a second go at this Donny asshole, whoever he was. It was clear the bastard had bothered her before—and that he'd been waiting for her, maybe even stalking her.

Nate had just climbed into the cab of his truck when he'd spotted the Lincoln Continental pull up behind her and a man jump out and rush into her car. Nate had reacted on instinct, leaving his truck in the alley and going after the bastard, his Colt M1911 cocked and locked in his concealed shoulder holster. He'd forgotten about the men in the car until the window had rolled down and he'd seen the barrel of a Glock pointed his way.

And you fought as a special operator for what branch of the military, West—the Salvation Army?

He'd been lucky those idiots couldn't shoot worth a damn.

It was dark now, the wind colder. Drivers slowed down as they passed, pedestrians stopping on the sidewalk to watch the spectacle of squad cars and flashing lights.

Nate's thoughts were interrupted by a child's giggle. He followed the sound, his gaze drawn to a tall man in a black SWAT uniform who carried a blond-haired little girl. Wearing a pink coat and wrapped in a white blanket, the girl must have been about four years old. The cop bounced her in his arms, and she giggled again, clutching a purple toy pony to her chin.

She was about the cutest thing Nate had ever seen.

Megan must have heard her daughter's laughter, too. Relief on her face, she got out of the car and hurried over to the man, who enfolded her in his embrace, kissing her cheek and placing the little girl—Megan had called her Emily—in her arms. Megan held her daughter close, tears spilling down her cheeks. The tall cop put his arms around her, holding both mother and daughter close. Was he her boyfriend? Her husband? Nate couldn't recall seeing a wedding ring on her finger.

And then suddenly he wanted nothing more than to get back to the ranch. Without saying goodbye, he crossed the street, climbed into his truck, and headed for home.

It was only after he was halfway there that he realized he had her wallet—the wallet he'd ripped from that bastard Donny's hands—in his coat pocket.

CHAPTER 2

"I want to be reassigned from SWAT to Megan's protection detail until we have this sonofabitch in custody. I don't give a shit if it's a conflict of interests."

Fighting to ignore the anxious knot in her stomach, Megan set about reheating last night's leftover spaghetti for Emily's supper, while Marc paced the living room talking on his cell phone with Chief Irving. No matter that Irving was Marc's boss and ought to have been the one giving orders. Marc was the most protective big brother in the history of the universe. He wouldn't let something like rank stand in his way.

Megan would never be able to repay Marc for all he'd done to keep her safe—nor would she ever be able to make up for the hurt she'd caused him.

She slid a plate of spaghetti and green beans in the microwave, pushed the buttons, then turned her back to the stove, feeling strangely disoriented in her own kitchen, her sense of safety shattered.

Damn it! Damn!

Why had she believed that a restraining order would be enough to keep Donny away? She should have realized that news stories about the settlement from her lawsuit against the state Department of Corrections would catch his attention. Though the total amount of the settlement—$1.5 million—was sealed by court order, Donny would know it involved a lot of money. He knew what had been done to her.

She closed her eyes and began to count, breathing deeply, trying to dissipate the panic that had begun to gather behind her breastbone.

"The witness put three forty-five rounds through that Continental. With any luck, some bastard is on his way to the ER with lead in his ass. We're canvassing ERs just in case. No, I didn't get to speak with the man, though I owe him a huge debt of thanks."

Megan's eyes opened, her brother's words bringing back those few crucial moments in the car.

Are you okay?

Y-yes, but the men in the other car—

Get down!

Bam! Bam! Bam!

Nathaniel West might well have saved her life tonight—and Emily's.

The microwave beeped, making Megan jump.

She drew a shaky breath. Willing herself to hold onto her composure for Emily's sake, she reached for her daughter, who sat on the floor coloring in her new horse coloring book. "Let's wash your hands, sweet pea."

She picked Emily up, carried her to the sink and helped her lather and rinse her hands, then sat her in her chair, placing the plate of spaghetti and green beans before her together with a small fork and a sippy cup of milk. She reached for a bib and was tying it around Emily's neck when someone came up behind her.

"What am I supposed to eat?"

Megan gasped and jumped, startled by the sound of her brother's voice. "I... I can make more spaghetti if you..."

"Megan." Marc's grin faded to a look of concern. He drew her into his arms and held her close. "I was kidding. The last thing in the world I want you to worry about tonight is feeding my face. I'll send one of the guys out to grab me a sandwich or something. You should eat, too."

"I'm not hungry." Megan let herself sink into her brother's embrace, hating herself for feeling so afraid again, so vulnerable. She'd tried to put all of this behind her for Emily's sake—and for her own. And now...

"I'm so, so sorry this happened." Marc drew back, looked into her eyes. "I promise I'm going to put him away so that he can't hurt you or threaten Emily again. I wish I'd blown his head off when I had the chance."

Megan drew away, shaking her head. "Don't say that. If you had, you'd probably still be in prison."

Marc raised a hand to the earpiece in his right ear, his gaze shifting toward the front door a moment before someone knocked. "It's about time."

Megan watched while Marc walked to the door and opened it to reveal Julian Darcangelo, his best friend and the only police officer other than her brother whom Megan trusted with her life. He was dressed head to toe in black as he usually was when he was working a case—black leather jacket, black turtleneck, black jeans, black boots—his dark hair tied back in a short ponytail.

"McBride is on his way." He exchanged a quick glance with Marc, then strolled into the kitchen. "How you doing, kiddo?"

Megan hugged her arms around herself, the concern and sympathy in Julian's eyes somehow making it harder not to cry. "I... I'm okay."

"Uncle Julie!" Emily squealed at the sight of him, her face lighting up, her smile messy with spaghetti sauce.

From the living room, Megan heard Marc snicker. "Uncle *Julie.*"

"Hey, sweetie." Julian flipped Marc off discreetly behind his back, gave Emily a warm smile, then met Megan's gaze, seeming to study her. "You need a hug?"

It was Julian's way of asking her whether it was okay for him to touch her. He had spent the better part of his years with the FBI working undercover to free girls and women who'd fallen victim to sex trafficking. He seemed to understand better than anyone how hard it was for her to trust men, to let them near her, to let them touch her, even in a casual way.

She nodded, tears blurring her vision.

He wrapped his arms around her. "It's going to be okay. Donny doesn't know it yet, but he just picked a fight with the wrong bunch of guys."

Nate knew it would have been easier to drop Megan's wallet by the police station and let the cops handle it. There was no need for him to deliver it in person. And yet, here he was, turning onto her street at the wheel of the damned delivery truck.

She lived in a tidy middle-class neighborhood with minivans in the driveways and strollers and bicycles on the porches—a family neighborhood. He glanced at the houses, saw that odd addresses were on the left side of the street, even ones on the right. And there it was—two houses down. High-grade security lights illuminated the yard all around, making the house stand out from its neighbors

He pulled up in front, parked at the curb, and climbed out of the truck, her wallet tucked in his jacket pocket, some part of him wondering what the hell he was doing here. The last thing Megan would want tonight is some stranger showing up at her door.

He started up the sidewalk, but hadn't taken ten steps when he heard heavy footfalls on the ground behind him.

"Freeze! Police!"

What the… ?

Nate stopped and slowly raised his hands, only to find himself rushed from all sides by men with weapons drawn. He opened his mouth to tell them he wasn't the man they were looking for, but was shouted down.

"Down on the ground! Hands behind your head!"

"You've got to be fucking kidding me." He did as they demanded, rough hands forcing him to the cold concrete, patting him down

A hand slid beneath Nate's parka and found his empty holster. "Shoulder holster, but no weapon. Where's the weapon, buddy? Did you leave it in the truck?"

Nate tried to explain. "The police confiscated—"

Another hand reached into his right jeans pocket. "He's got her wallet."

"You son of a bitch!"

"Back off, Hunter. You're too close to this. Let us handle it."

"You're making a mistake. I'm Nathaniel West. I was at the scene today. I'm the one who—"

Strong hands grasped Nate's wrists, bringing his arms behind his back, making the constricted muscles and tendons in his right shoulder and arm scream.

Gritting his teeth against the pain, Nate tried again. "I'm Nathaniel West—the man who called 911. I'm the one who got that bastard Donny off her."

Cold plastic gripped his wrists as the cuffs were drawn tight.

"Nathaniel West?" asked the man who had just cuffed him. "Got proof of that?"

"Yes." Sweat beaded on Nate's forehead, the pain in his shoulder unrelenting. He rested his cheek on the cold sidewalk, willed his arm to relax. "My wallet is in the truck."

"I'm on it." Footsteps on concrete. The squeak of the truck door's hinges. The clank as the door was shut again. "His driver's license says Nathaniel West. Is that the guy's name, Hunter?"

"Shit. Yeah, McBride. That's his name."

"What are you doing here?" came the voice from the man holding Nate down.

"I came to give Ms. Hunter her wallet. I got it away from that son of a bitch when he and I fought, but I forgot I had it. Now, can you get me out of these damned cuffs? You know I'm not armed."

"We've got the wrong man." That was the voice of the cop who'd gone to the truck. "Let him up, Darcangelo."

Nate felt a tug on the plastic as the cuffs were cut and his wrists were freed. He pushed himself up with his left arm and got to his feet, rubbing the ache from his right shoulder. He glanced around and found himself surrounded by three men, all of them as tall as he was, a few uniforms hanging out in the background.

Darcangelo—the one who'd held him down and cuffed him—wore a black leather jacket and jeans, his hair drawn back in a ponytail. The lack of badge and street clothes told Nate he was a detective. He looked like a man who'd spent his life on the street and knew how to fight dirty. His relaxed stance didn't fool Nate. The man was like a cougar, ready to attack.

Beside Darcangelo stood a clean-cut man wearing a suit and tie, a duty badge that read "Chief Deputy U.S. Marshal Zach McBride" clipped on his jacket. McBride studied Nate with a gaze that could cut glass, then glanced at Nate's driver's license. "Definitely the wrong guy."

A SWAT cop, a police detective and a chief deputy U.S. Marshal made for a very unusual surveillance team. He'd bet they were buddies.

Nate reached out, took his wallet. "Damned right you got the wrong guy. Don't you think you went a bit overboard? You could've at least asked my name before you shoved me to the ground."

"Sorry, but I take no chances where Megan is concerned." Hunter, the SWAT cop Nate recognized from the crime scene, stepped forward, Megan's wallet in his left hand. He offered Nate his right. "Marc Hunter with Denver SWAT. Thanks for what you did today. You may have saved my sister's life."

His *sister*?

Megan was his sister.

And suddenly Nate felt less like kicking the man's ass.

He took Hunter's hand, gave as firm a shake as he got, ignoring the pain in his scarred fingers and tendons. "I'm glad I was able to help."

The front door opened and Megan appeared, her face illuminated by the porch light. And, man, did she look angry. "Marc, stop! He's the man… Oh. You figured that out."

"I told you to stay away from the windows." Hunter glared at his sister.

She ignored him, her gaze meeting Nate's, her expression softening. "I… I'm sorry. My brother is just trying to keep me safe."

"I brought your wallet." Nate found it hard to talk with her looking at him like that. "I got it away from Donny and then forgot it was in my pocket."

Hunter handed the wallet to his sister. "At least Donny doesn't have it—which means he and his gang might not know where you live."

Megan looked down at the wallet, then back at Nate. "Won't you come inside, Nathaniel?"

"Call me Nate." He needed to hit the road. He had a long drive home, and he needed to take care of the graze on his shoulder. Besides, he had no business getting involved with a woman right now—particularly when that woman's brother was as protective as a pit bull and traveled with a pack.

But his mouth didn't seem to be listening to his brain. "Thanks. I'd like that."

Megan led Nate inside and shut the door behind him, ignoring the surprise on Marc's face. She'd wanted to kick her brother's butt when she'd realized who it was he and Julian had pinned to the ground in handcuffs. It was one thing to watch the house. It was another to beat up every man who tried to come to her door.

"Can I take your coat?" She glanced around, feeling suddenly conscious of the toys on the living room floor, the thin layer of dust on the furniture, and her own less than polished appearance. She probably had mascara all over her face from crying, not to mention her bruised and swollen cheek.

For a moment, he looked like he would refuse. "Sure. Thanks."

He shrugged out of the shearling barn jacket, wincing slightly as he drew out his left arm. His dark blue long-sleeved T-shirt was torn at the shoulder, and the cloth was stained with …

Blood.

"Oh, God! I forgot you were hit!"

"It's nothing, really." He looked down at her, his gaze fixed on the bruise on her cheek. "Just a minor graze."

"I'll clean it for you."

He shook his head. "I can deal with it when I get home."

"Don't be silly." She walked into the kitchen, needing to check on Emily. "It's the least I can do."

He followed.

Back in the kitchen, Emily had finished her spaghetti and was sipping milk from her cup, her fingers as messy as her face, her fork conveniently forgotten.

"This is my little girl, Emily." Megan couldn't help but smile as she looked over at her daughter. Emily was the greatest blessing of her life, the one pure and beautiful thing that Megan had done, the only reason she didn't view her entire life as a terrible mistake.

If a little girl as sweet and innocent as Emily had come from inside her, then she couldn't be all that bad.

Nate looked over at Emily and smiled. "Hi, Emily. I'm Nate."

Emily dropped her cup and put her hands over her face, hiding.

"I guess she's going to be shy now. Sorry." Megan walked to the sink, got a wash cloth wet with warm water. "We don't get many visitors apart from family."

"No worries." A chair scraped the floor as Nate sat down at the table. "How old are you, Emily?"

Megan turned in time to see Emily take one hand from her face and hold up four messy little fingers.

"Four! You're getting to be a big girl, aren't you?"

Emily covered her face again and nodded from behind her mask.

"You're good with kids. Do you have children of your own?" Megan walked to the table, wash cloth in hand, and wiped the spaghetti sauce off Emily's hands and face. This naturally made Emily squirm in protest.

"No, no kids. I've never been married."

Neither had Megan. She lifted Emily to the floor. "Why don't you finish coloring your pretty picture while Mommy and Nate talk?"

Emily flopped down on her tummy, picked up a red crayon and began to color the horse's mane, humming sweetly to herself, her feet in the air.

And then it hit Megan as it hadn't before.

Emily had been in danger today—because of her.

Oh, my God! Emily! They're going after my little girl!

Call the cops. They'll get to her faster than you can.

Feeling as if she were made of wood, Megan walked back to the sink with the dirty wash cloth. She washed her hands, then turned to find Nate watching her. "Thank you for calling 911, for staying calm when I panicked. Your quick thinking helped keep my daughter safe."

If anything should ever happen to Emily…

"You've had a rough night." His voice was deep, soothing, his blue eyes warm as he watched her.

If the right side of his face weren't so terribly scarred, he would have been almost frighteningly handsome. His jaw was square, his lips set in a firm line, his eyes expressive. He was every bit as tall as Marc, with broad shoulders and thick sandy brown hair that he'd cropped short. Although his right hand was badly scarred, his left was unhurt, his nails neatly trimmed.

"Yeah." She looked away, surprised to find herself thinking of him as a *man*—and yet feeling at ease with him at the same time. It must be because he'd saved her life. "It would have been a lot rougher if you hadn't showed up when you did."

"I'm glad I was there." The tone of his voice told her that he meant it. "The guy who attacked you—has he been stalking you?"

"Yeah." She couldn't bring herself to tell Nate the whole truth about Donny.

"I know your brother is watching out for you, but maybe you should consider getting a concealed carry permit and a little revolver to keep in your purse—just in case."

"I… don't feel comfortable with firearms." Another half-truth.

The whole truth was that, in addition to her aversion to guns, she couldn't legally own or posses a firearm, much less qualify for concealed carry.

"If you wanted to learn how to shoot, I'd be happy to give you lessons. I bet your brother would be willing to help you out, too."

"Thanks. I'll talk to Marc about it." She hoped Nate would let it go. "Are you hungry? Can I get you something to eat or drink?"

"Water's good."

She got out a clean glass, filled it with water and ice from the dispenser in her fridge door. While he drank, she retrieved her first aid kit from the cupboard above the stove. "You'll need to take off your shirt."

He set the nearly empty glass aside. "You don't need to do this."

"You didn't need to help me either." She turned toward him, first-aid kit in hand, her gaze meeting his. "You could've turned your back and driven away, but you didn't. You helped me even though I was a stranger. It almost got you killed. I'd like to help you in some small way—if you'll let me."

Seeming to hesitate, he stood, grasped the hem of his shirt and slowly drew it up over his belly and chest. The left side of his body, like the left side of his face, was stirringly male—an honest-to-God six pack, a well defined chest, muscular arms, a scattering of soft brown curls, a flat, dark nipple. But the right side was horribly scarred from the waistline of his jeans up to his shoulder—no nipple, no chest hair.

He was half marble sculpture, half tortured survivor. The thought of how much he must have suffered gave Megan chills.

She set the first-aid kit on the table and took a good look at the wound in his left shoulder. It was deeper than she had imagined it would be and caked with dried blood. If the round had struck him only six inches more to the right, he'd be dead. "I'm so sorry this happened. It must be painful."

He turned his head, looked down at his own shoulder. "It's nothing, really."

Compared to what he'd been through, it probably *was* nothing.

She opened the kit, slipped on a pair of sterile nitrile gloves, and reached for a packet of Lidocaine gel. "This will numb it so I can clean it without hurting you."

"That's one heck of a first-aid kit. You a nurse?"

"No." She opened the packet and squeezed the gel onto the wound, gently rubbing it in. "It was a housewarming gift from one of my brother's friends. Gabe is a paramedic. He taught me how to use everything. He wanted me to be prepared."

"Your brother has some good friends. Those guys out front— they're part of his crew, too, aren't they?"

"Yes." She couldn't help but smile. Marc's friends had become her extended family. They knew the truth about her, but they still cared about her. If that wasn't the definition of family, what was? "They're kind of like a big brother posse."

"I believe it."

She looked up to find Nate watching her, stepped back, and tossed the empty gel packet in the trash. "Now we wait."

CHAPTER 3

Nate hadn't bared any part of his body to a woman who wasn't a nurse since he'd been burned. He felt naked now, exposed to the gaze of a woman who was little more than a stranger. And yet Megan hadn't balked at the sight of him, hadn't looked away, hadn't tried to cover up her own unease with nervous conversation. She'd looked straight at him and then had gotten to work. "You haven't asked me."

The pain in his shoulder began to fade, the gel doing its job.

She reached into the first-aid kit for a Betadine packet. "Asked you about what?"

"How I got burned."

She opened the packet, poured Betadine into one side of it, dipping the gauze into the antiseptic solution. "I guess you'd tell me if you wanted me to know."

"I was caught by an IED."

"So you were a soldier." She cleaned the skin around the wound, washing away dried blood.

"I was a Marine special operator." He tried not to notice the way his abdominal muscles tensed when she touched him. "Our convoy got hit in Kandahar Province."

She tossed the bloodied gauze into the trash, reached for another pad, and dipped it into the Betadine, this time washing the wound itself. "That's in Afghanistan, right?"

"Yeah. The blast ignited the fuel tank." He was sharing the worst memory of his life, and yet all he could think about was the woman beside him. What the hell was up with that? "Three men died instantly. Six of us were badly wounded."

Her hands stilled, and she looked at him through green eyes full of shadows—too many shadows for a woman in her twenties. "I'm sorry. It must have been terrible. Losing friends, the physical pain. I can't imagine it."

Her sincerity touched him, made his mind go blank. He managed to say something in response. "We knew the risks when we signed on."

"Yes, but no one thinks it will happen to them. Then, when it does... "

The resignation in her voice told him she spoke from personal experience, and he found himself wondering what had happened to her.

She reached for another clean piece of gauze, dipped it in the antiseptic, and cleaned deeper this time. "Does this hurt?"

"No." He felt no pain, but he *was* feeling her.

He seemed to be aware of everything about her. The feminine timbre of her voice. The soft scent of her skin. The curves of her ass and hips beneath the soft cloth of her jeans. The swells of her breasts beneath her sweater. The loving way she looked over at her daughter every couple of minutes, keeping a watchful eye. The gentleness of her fingers against his skin.

Even through the sterile gloves, her touch seared him.

How long had it been since he'd been with a woman?

He'd been faithful to Rachel the entire time he'd been downrange, so with the time he'd spent in the hospital, that meant three years, almost four.

Too damned long.

"Thank you for your service—and your sacrifice." Megan tossed the piece of dirty gauze in the trash. "And here you are injured again—this time helping me. You've got it, you know."

"Got what?"

"The hero gene." She reached for a large adhesive bandage, peeled off the paper wrapping and the tabs, and pressed it gently over his wound. "It's the gene that drives some men to act and take responsibility while others do nothing."

Nate had always thought that had to do with balls, not genetics, but he didn't say that, not with that sweet little girl with the big blue eyes who was sitting just a few feet away.

And then it hit him.

Where was Emily's father?

He glanced around the kitchen, saw nothing masculine, no work gloves left on the counter, no man's lunch box, no family photos— nothing to indicate that anyone other than Megan and her daughter lived in the house. That helped explain why her brother was so damned protective. If Nate had a little sister, and she lived alone with a child and was being stalked, he would probably act like a pit bull, too.

"This ought to at least help prevent infection. You should have your doctor look at it."

"Thanks." He glanced down at the bandage, his gaze following Megan as she removed the gloves and tossed them in the trash.

No wedding ring.

The front door opened and closed, and Megan's brother appeared in the kitchen. He took one look at Nate standing there shirtless, and his eyes narrowed, his gaze traveling over Nate's torso—and his scars. "What the... ?"

"Nate was shot in the fight with Donny." Megan gave her brother a look that quite clearly told him to back down. "I offered to clean and bandage the wound."

Nate flexed his shoulder. The bandage held. "You did a good job of it, too. Thank you."

"It's the least I can do." Megan shut the first-aid kit and carried it back to the cupboard. "Are you hungry? I've got leftover spaghetti. I can reheat a plate in the microwave."

"No, thanks." Nate really needed to get back to the ranch.

"See, Mommy? See, Uncle Marc?" Emily got to her feet and held up her coloring book to reveal a drawing of a mare and foal covered in bold squiggles of brown, pink, and blue. "I drawed horsies. There's a mommy and a baby."

"Show me."

Nate watched as Megan knelt down, giving Emily her full attention as if this one drawing were the most important thing in her world. She obviously loved her daughter with every fiber of her being. And Nate found himself wanting to beat the shit out of the man who had brought violence to Megan's world and fear to her heart.

What kind of animal could threaten a mother's child?

"Can I have a horsie, Mommy?"

Megan stood, shaking her head. "Not in the city, sweet pea. Our yard wouldn't be big enough for a horse."

"Bring her up to the Cimarron sometime." The words were out before Nate realized he'd spoken. "We breed quarter horses. If there's snow, I'll hook up the sleigh, and we'll go for a sleigh ride."

For a guy who's not ready to get involved with a woman, you're sure involving yourself, West. A sleigh ride?

"I suppose you're anxious to get back on the road." Hunter's message was unmistakable and as subtle as a grenade. He wanted Nate to leave. Clearly the idea of Nate spending any time with Megan had raised his hackles.

But Nate wasn't going anywhere just yet.

He took his wallet out of his pocket, and pulled out one of the Cimarron's business cards. "The mares will be foaling come March. Call any time."

Megan took the card, glanced at it. The words "Cimarron Ranch" were spelled out in embossed brick red in a font that was evocative of the Wild West, a C and R back to back in the upper left corner. The ranch's brand? Nate's name, phone number and address ran along the bottom. She looked up at him. "Thanks. For everything."

"You're welcome." He grinned, his scars seeming to vanish in the brightness of his smile and the warmth in his eyes. "Like I said, I'm just glad I was there."

Megan's pulse skipped, something fluttering deep in her belly.

Was she attracted to him?

Oh, God!

She was.

It was even more of a jolt to realize that he was attracted to her, too. And for a moment, she could do nothing but stand there, looking into his eyes.

A tug at her leg drew Megan back to the moment. "Can we see the horsies, Mommy? Can we go see horsies?"

It took Megan a moment to find her tongue, her heart racing, astonishment and panic tangled inside her. "Uh… Yeah, maybe. We'll see, sweet pea."

She risked eye contact again and found him still watching her.

If he knew the truth about her, about the things she'd done and the life she'd led, he'd turn his back on her. It didn't matter that she'd worked hard for years to rebuild her life, getting clean, going to college, holding down a job, winning back custody of Emily from the state. In his eyes, she would be permanently damaged goods.

There were some things the world simply didn't forgive.

Nate's gaze shifted to Marc. "Is there any way you can help expedite the return of my firearm? I've got other handguns at home, but the Colt is my favorite and fits my shoulder holster best."

Marc seemed to consider it. "I'll see what I can do."

"I suggested Megan get a concealed carry permit and offered to teach her to shoot, but I guess she's not comfortable with firearms."

Marc covered for her smoothly. "Yeah, she really hates guns, but she'll be under police protection until we catch this bastard. I'll walk out with you."

It was all Megan could do not to roll her eyes at her brother.

Nate closed his hand over Megan's, gave it a squeeze, sending sparks of awareness skittering up her arm. "Take care, Megan. Stay safe. Thanks for fixing up my shoulder. The invitation to visit the ranch is an open one."

"You're welcome." Megan surprised herself again by returning the squeeze. "And thanks. What you did today…"

He released her hand at last. "I did what any man would do."

Megan knew from experience that wasn't true.

"Your jacket." She hurried to the coat closet, took it from its hanger, and handed it to him. "It's cold outside."

"Thanks. Goodnight."

"Goodnight." She watched as Marc left with Nate through the front door, then hurried to the window and peeked through the blinds. Julian and Zach stood near Nate's truck, an unmarked squad car parked down the street with a couple of uniforms inside. Julian and Zach turned toward Marc and Nate, both shaking Nate's hand in turn before heading to Julian's pickup, leaving Marc and Nate alone.

What was Marc saying? He was probably threatening Nate with bodily harm if he came anywhere near her again. He ought to thank the man. If it hadn't been for Nate…

Behind her, Emily was playing with her favorite toy pony.

Nate's business card still in hand, Megan sank legless onto the couch, feeling overwhelmed. First Donny, and then this.

She took twenty deep, slow breaths, but the sense of calm she so desperately needed evaded her, images from the evening invading her mind, one colliding with the next. Donny hopped up on meth, tossing Emily's photo as if she meant nothing to him. Nate appearing out of nowhere, dragging Donnie out of the car. Nate firing his gun, asking her if she was okay. Marc arriving at the scene, Emily in his arms. Nate standing shirtless in her kitchen. Nate looking down at her, that handsome smile on his face.

Her eyes opened.

She tossed Nate's business card onto the coffee table. She had no room for a man in her life, not now, not when she was so close to putting the pieces together. Even if she'd wanted to get to know Nate better, he would lose interest in her the moment he knew the truth about her. What was the point of starting down that road?

Although this was supposed to be a new beginning for her, there really wasn't any such thing as starting over. The past still followed her everywhere. It had dogged her through two years of college. It had come with her to every job interview. And it had been with her tonight when Nate had asked about Donny, when he'd suggested she learn to shoot, even when he'd smiled at her.

An ache formed in her chest, sharp and hollow. No matter how much she wanted to know what it was like to love a man and be loved by him, to be the center of his world, to feel safe and at home in his arms, she knew it would never happen. Even if she found a man who could forgive her past, she didn't think she'd ever be able to enjoy being touched, having sex.

What man could love a woman who wouldn't let him touch her?

Emily galloped her pony across the couch cushions.

Feeling empty, Megan stood, willing herself to think only of her daughter. "It's time for your bath, sweet pea."

She'd just gotten Emily dried off and into her favorite fuzzy pink jammies when Marc walked inside. She glared up at him. "You didn't have to be so rough to Nate, you know? You probably hurt him. I'm sure those burns go deep."

Marc frowned. "You like him."

"He may have saved my life—and Emily's. Of course I like him."

Marc's eyes narrowed. "That's not what I meant, and you know it."

Megan said nothing.

"I did a background check. No arrests. He fought with the Marines, made first lieutenant and was decorated more than once. He was honorably discharged after—"

"You ran a background check on the man who saved my life?" Megan stared at her brother, stunned that he'd gone so far. "Isn't that a bit extreme?"

"Just because he played the hero today doesn't mean he is one. He could be anyone, Megan. I needed to know." Marc turned and knelt down before Emily. "How would you like me to read you a bedtime story?"

Emily nodded and smiled.

"Go pick out your favorite storybooks, and I'll be right there."

Megan watched Emily scamper down the hallway toward her bedroom.

"I'll take care of Emily," Marc said quietly. "Why don't you go fill up the tub, soak, and relax? This has been a tough night for you all around, and you've handled it well—too well."

Megan shook her head, crossed her arms over her chest, tears stinging her eyes. "I feel like a total wreck."

"From where I stand, you're doing great." Marc hugged her close. "There was a time when you would've turned to the needle. Give yourself some credit."

She nodded, looked into her brother's eyes. "Thanks."

"You're welcome." He released her, his voice taking on a reassuring tone. "There's nothing to worry about tonight. We've got surveillance outside, and I'm staying the night on your couch."

And just like that Megan regretted being angry with her brother. He was only trying to protect her, after all. "What would I do without you?"

"Hey, I lived half my life without you, Megan. I'm not about to let a crazy asshole like Donny hurt my little sister. Now go rest while I spoil my niece."

"You did the right thing." The old man put his empty scotch glass down on the end table, his long legs stretched out before the fire. "I've got no tolerance for a man who hurts women or children. Every man on this planet owes his life to a woman. I hope they catch the bastard and hang him by his nuts."

Jack West had never been one to mince words. A lifelong rancher and Vietnam veteran, he was unflinchingly honest and took shit from no one. That was one of many reasons Nate respected his father.

"I invited Megan to bring her little girl, Emily, to the ranch to see the horses. The kid loves horses."

One gray eyebrow arched.

"What?" Nate's eyes narrowed.

"Sounds like there might be something going on here."

"Nothing's going on. That's wishful thinking."

For the past six months, his father had been pushing him to get out and meet women, but Nate didn't want to put himself on the meat market. He wasn't ready for that yet.

"You don't so much as mention a woman for two years. Then you save this young lady's life, drive her wallet to her house so you can deliver it in person, and invite her to bring her child to the ranch. Sounds like something's going on."

"Get your hearing checked."

Irritated, Nate got up, walked to the fireplace, and jabbed at the embers, tossing a few more big pieces of hardwood on the blaze. There was nothing going on between him and Megan Hunter. Yes, there was something special about her, something that had caught his eye, something that had made him look forward to seeing her at the shelter. What he'd seen tonight—her love for her daughter, her concern for him—had deepened his attraction. But he hadn't rushed in to help her because he wanted to get involved with her. He'd have done the same thing if she'd been a blue-haired old lady. Besides, inviting her to bring her four-year-old to the ranch to look at horses wasn't exactly asking her out on a date.

And what about the part where she touched you through sterile gloves and you turned into mush? Remember that part?

So he had some pent-up testosterone. So what? Any man who'd spent almost four years fucking nothing but his own fist would.

He walked back to the couch, sank into the leather cushions, and reached for his scotch, taking a deep drink.

"Sooner or later, son, you're going to have to put Rachel behind you and take a chance again. You're a young man, and you're going to want more in your life than this ranch and horses—a wife, a couple of kids."

"Dad, stop. I don't want to talk about it."

"You never want to talk about it."

"Mom has been gone for five years now." She'd died suddenly of an aneurysm while Nate had been downrange in Afghanistan. He'd gotten a call from his father in the middle of the night and had managed to get emergency leave to return to Colorado for her funeral. His father had seemed to age a decade that day. "Would you like to talk about why *you're* not out meeting women?"

The old man glared at him. "That's different. Your mother and I were married for the better part of forty years. We had a life together. We had the ranch. We had you. Rachel was just your fiancée. You never even lived together."

"This doesn't have a damn thing to do with Rachel."

That same eyebrow arched. "Doesn't it?"

For a moment, neither of them spoke.

Stubbornness was a quality they both had—in spades.

"What did you say her brother's name was?"

"Marc Hunter. Marc with a 'c.' He's with Denver SWAT."

"Marc Hunter." The old man frowned. "Why does that name sound so familiar?"

Nate shrugged. "No clue."

His father drained the last of his scotch, then got to his feet. "I'm putting these old bones to bed. Morning comes early. We'll be doing body condition scoring on bred cows from the north herd tomorrow, and we've got a shipment of hay coming in."

"I'll handle the hay." It would give Nate a chance to work his arm, shoulder, and chest muscles again.

If his father had any reservations about giving the more physical chore to Nate, he didn't show it. He gave a nod. "You better hit the sack, too."

But it was a long time before Nate was able to sleep, his mind on a woman with auburn hair and shadows in her wide, green eyes.

CHAPTER 4

Megan unfastened the safety strap on Emily's car seat and lifted her daughter out of the vehicle, grabbing the lunch she'd packed for her. "Hold my hand, sweet pea."

She crossed the parking lot as quickly as Emily's little legs would allow, her gaze searching among the cars in the parking lot, along the street, and among the trees near the little Montessori center's entrance for any sign of the Lincoln Continental, for men she didn't know, for Donny. An unmarked police car had followed her all the way from home, but Megan still had a hard time trusting cops, apart from her brother and Julian.

Almost a week had gone by since Donny had ambushed her, and the police had found no sign of him. They hadn't found the Lincoln Continental either. Although Megan was under surveillance all day, she couldn't shake the sense that something terrible was going to happen.

Inside the preschool it was warm—and noisy.

Christa, the head teacher, greeted them at the door and took Emily's lunch. "Good morning, Emily! Are you ready to have a fun day?"

Emily nodded, a shy smile on her face, her little ponytail bobbing.

Megan signed her daughter in, helped her out of her coat, and went to hang the coat in Emily's cubby. There was a manila envelope sitting on the shelf where the teachers put Emily's drawings, paperwork, and the school's monthly newsletter. She grabbed it, tucked it under her arm, and knelt down to kiss Emily good-bye.

"Have a good day, sweet pea." She hugged Emily close, finding it hard to let her go. "I'll see you this afternoon. Can you be a good girl for Christa?"

Emily nodded, smiled again.

"She's always a good girl, aren't you, Emily?" Christa guided Emily through the baby gate toward the play area, turning back toward Megan. "How are you holding up?"

Christa had been the one to take the call from the police that night. She'd locked the center down until Marc had arrived to claim Emily. Megan would always be grateful for her caution and quick action.

Megan willed herself to smile. "I'm doing alright, I guess. It scares me to be away from her all day."

Christa rested her hand on Megan's arm and gave her a reassuring squeeze. "I promise I won't let her out of my sight."

"Thank you." Megan glanced over at Emily, who was already lost in play with a group of girls who were setting up a little tea party for a handful of very lucky stuffed animals.

She loved the easy way Emily blended in with the other children—something Megan had never been able to do, before she'd been adopted out or after.

She turned to go, reaching into her coat pocket for her keys. The manila envelope that she'd tucked under her arm and forgotten fell on the floor. She reached down to get it and froze, her heart thudding.

On the front there was no postage, no date stamp, no address, just a number written with black marker: 143280.

Her inmate number.

Megan stared at it, children's voices fading around her, her pulse thrumming in her ears. Very few people had had access to that number—Marc, his wife, Sophie, her parole officer, and Donny. She picked the envelope up, her hands shaking as she opened it.

Inside was a hand-written note—and photographs. The photos, taken this week, showed her outside the daycare center taking Emily home for the night, at the grocery store, walking into her own home, gassing up the car.

Adrenaline punched through her, making her mouth go dry.

If they could take photos of her with Emily outside her own home and sneak them into the preschool with cops parked nearby…

She glanced at the note—instructions on where to put a hundred thousand dollars and threats to harm both her and Emily if she didn't.

Megan turned to Christa, interrupting her conversation with another mother. "Someone brought this inside and left it in Emily's cubby. Who was it? When?"

She handed the note to Christa, whose face paled as she read it. "You found this *here*?"

"It was in Emily's cubby. Someone delivered it in person. Look—no stamps." Megan showed Christa the envelope, amazed that she sounded so calm when, inside, she wanted to scream. "Come, Emily, sweet pea. We need to go."

She hurried Emily to the car and drove straight to the police station.

Nate piled slices of leftover roast beef on a hard roll, added mayonnaise, mustard, a slice of cheddar cheese, sliced tomato, avocado, lettuce, and a chopped jalapeño pepper, then took his sandwich and a bottle of Fat Tire to the table. He'd gotten the hay off the semi, storing some of it in the barn and loading some of it onto a truck so that it could be driven out to pasture. It had been hard work, making his arm, chest, and shoulder ache, but it had been satisfying, too. He'd worked up a sweat—and an appetite.

He reached for the paper only to find his father had already cut it to pieces. The old man was a pack rat who clipped and saved news stories he found interesting. That was all fine and good, but it made it damned hard to read the paper unless Nate got to it first. At least the sports section was still intact.

Nate read while he ate, wishing it were still baseball season. He was reading predictions for the Mile High Showdown—the annual contest between the CU Buffs and the CSU Rams—when the old man walked up to the table with a thick manila folder and dropped it on the table in front of Nate. "*This* is why the name Marc Hunter sounded familiar to me."

"Are you still going on about that?" It had been almost a week, but the old man still refused to let it go.

His dad sat, a mug of coffee in his hand. "I think you need to see it."

Nate took a bite of his sandwich, opened the folder—and almost choked.

There on top of a pile of newspaper clippings sat a wanted poster with an image of Marc Hunter. His hair was down to his shoulders, and he was sporting a beard and mustache, but the man was unmistakably Megan's brother. If visual proof hadn't been enough, the name "Marc Hunter" was prominent on the poster—not far from the words "armed and dangerous."

Megan's brother was an ex-con?

Some part of Nate wanted to laugh.

"This story broke about four years go. I followed it pretty closely because Hunter took that woman reporter hostage and fled into the mountains. They launched the biggest manhunt in the state's history to try to bring him in and rescue her. The men and I checked outbuildings and campsites on our land regularly for a month, but found no sign of him. Turns out there was a lot more to the story than anyone knew. It seems Hunter and his sister have had a pretty tough time of it. It's all there."

But Nate was already reading.

He didn't notice when his father stood and walked away.

Megan cut Emily's bean burrito into bite-size pieces, put the carrot sticks on the plate beside it, and set the plate on the coffee table in Marc's office, together with a plastic fork and napkin. "Thanks, Sophie. This is so much healthier than a hamburger from down the street. Can you thank Aunt Sophie for bringing us lunch, Emily?"

"Thank you, Auntie Sophie," Emily said in a small voice, smiling up at Sophie.

Sophie bent down, planted a kiss on Emily's head. "You're welcome, baby doll."

Megan had so many reasons to be grateful to Sophie. Before Sophie had become Megan's sister-in-law, she'd launched an investigation into the lives of pregnant women in prison. Her work had changed their lives—Marc's and Emily's as much as Megan's.

Megan had spent the morning sitting in Marc's office at police headquarters answering questions, while a team of detectives was dispatched to Emily's preschool. So far they'd found nothing—no sign of forced entry, no one at the daycare who noticed Donny or any other unauthorized people entering or leaving the daycare facility. Nor did they have any leads on the photographs—who had taken them or how someone had managed to follow her while she was under police surveillance without the cops noticing anything.

But Megan thought she knew the answer—or a least part of it.

Although Marc had reassured her that the men Chief Irving had assigned to watch over her could be trusted, Megan didn't believe it. She knew more than most people how easy it was for villains to masquerade as heroes, disguising the evil inside them with a uniform.

Sophie gave her a sympathetic look. "You haven't been sleeping, have you?"

Megan shook her head. "Not much."

"I know you don't want the newspaper to do a story on this, but I think—"

The office door opened and Marc walked in, shutting the door behind him. "Hey, honey. This is a nice surprise."

He leaned down and kissed Sophie, who grabbed the front of his shirt and held him down, drawing out the kiss, eliciting a deep "mmm" from her husband.

Their happiness and love for one another had always touched Megan. After everything he'd been through, her brother deserved someone wonderful in his life. They seemed made for each other.

And if Megan wished she knew what that kind of love was like…

She had so much for which she was grateful. She shouldn't waste time wishing for things that just couldn't happen.

Sophie smiled up at Marc. "The judge called for a recess in the trial I'm covering, so I brought Megan and Emily lunch."

"That was sweet of you." Marc turned to Megan. "We have a lead. It turns out the janitor put the envelope in the box. He was wearing cleaning gloves so he didn't leave prints. He said a man came up to the door early in the morning, said he had something to give you, and drew out a wad of cash, threatening to shoot—"

Megan shook her head, gave a nod toward Emily.

"Threatening to S-H-O-O-T the janitor if he mentioned anything about it. I've got to give Darcangelo credit. He's the one who got the man to talk."

"So Donny paid the janitor to put it in the cubby?"

"Not Donny." Marc leaned back against the wall. "The janitor described the man as heavy-set with dark hair and gold teeth. We've got him looking at mug shots now. I'm guessing this guy drives a Lincoln Continental or knows someone who does."

"Well, that's something," Sophie said, giving Marc's hand a squeeze.

"What do I do?" Megan fought to keep the panic out of her voice. "They want a hundred thousand dollars by ten tonight. You saw the note. You know what they'll try to do if they don't get it. I guess I need to go to the bank."

"Like hell you will." Marc crossed his arms over his chest. "You're going to go home with a police escort. You're going to pack suitcases for yourself and Emily, and I'm going to pick you up after work and take you to my place. You and Emily are going to stay with us until these guys are in custody. We'll take care of the rest."

Megan shook her head. "I have to go to work. It took me so long to find this job. They're depending on me. If I can't come in for two weeks or a month, they'll fire me. He's going to destroy my life, Marc. Donny is going to destroy everything I've worked so hard to build."

Marc knelt down in front of her, took her hands, and looked straight into her eyes. "That's not going to happen, Megan. You call your boss, tell her what's going on. I'll give her the damned police report if she wants it. As for the rest of it, we've got this. Trust me, okay?"

Megan drew a deep breath, nodded. "Okay."

Megan pulled into her driveway, Emily asleep in the back seat. An unmarked police car followed behind her, while another was already parked a few houses down. She recognized Detective Wu—one of Julian's most trusted men—in the front seat. She pushed the button to open her garage, pulled slowly inside, and closed the garage again.

And for a moment she simply sat there.

Her brother wanted her to trust the police, but Megan couldn't. If even one of them were corrupt, her brother wouldn't be able to protect her. Besides, having them follow her everywhere felt like being on parole or in prison again.

She carried Emily inside, laid her down on her bed, then began to pack. She'd called her boss, who'd been surprisingly understanding and told her to take the day off. Megan had been so grateful.

Marc was coming by at about seven tonight to pick her up and take her to his place. He hadn't told her the details, but she knew they had plans to catch Donny and the others tonight using a woman police detective in an auburn wig to make the money drop in her place. If it worked, Donny and the others would be in custody by morning, and this nightmare would be behind her. All she had to do was sit tight—and hope the men in the cars outside weren't working for the men who'd threatened her.

She finished packing her suitcase, packed one for Emily, and carried them both to the living room, catching sight of the squad car outside. She drew the blinds and sank onto the couch, feeling trapped.

And there on the coffee table she saw Nate's business card.

Nate showered off the hay dust and shaved, unable to shake the sick feeling in the pit of his stomach—or his rage. He'd heard of some pretty sick shit happening to women when he'd been deployed, and what had happened to Megan ranked right up there with the worst of it. But what had been done to Megan had happened right here in his country, in his home state, not in Afghanistan.

That poor girl has been through enough, I mean to tell you.

It all made sense now—the reverend's words, the shadows in her eyes, her fear of guns, why her brother was so damned protective. He still couldn't believe what Marc Hunter had done for his sister. It had been wrong—no question about that—but Nate could understand why he'd done it. He's paid one hell of a high price for it in the end.

There'd been photos of Megan, part of a series of stories about pregnant women in prison that had run in the Denver Independent.

She'd been Megan Rawlings back then, and she'd looked like a different person—haunted, fragile, unhealthy. Among them had been a series of shots that had put an ache in his chest.

Megan in labor while shackled to a hospital bed by her ankle, in pain and chained like an animal. Megan, still shackled by her ankle, looking down at newborn Emily, looking exhausted but happy. Megan in tears as her baby was taken away, despair on her face.

Nate didn't know what it was like to be a woman, or to bring a child into the world, or to have that child taken away. He'd never been arrested, had never spent a day in prison. He'd never been addicted to anything, not even the painkillers they'd pumped into his system when he'd been in the burn center. But he *did* know that it had taken a lot of guts for Megan to get from where she'd been in those photographs to where she was today.

And now some piece of shit was stalking her, threatening her, threatening little Emily. It made Nate want to hurt someone.

Specifically, Donny Lee Thomas.

Nate dried off, strode naked to his closet, and slipped into a pair of jeans. He'd just pulled a T-shirt over his head when his cell phone rang. He picked it up, glanced at the display, but didn't recognize the number. "Nate West."

"It's Megan. Megan Hunter."

"Megan." Nate felt guilt slide through him. He'd just spent the past hour reading her life story, and she didn't know it. "What's up?"

"I wondered if you'd mind very much if I brought Emily out to see the horses. You said it was an open invitation. But maybe you're busy." There was hesitation in her voice, as if she expected him to say "no." Beneath that, he heard fear.

"Has something happened?"

She hesitated. "I found a letter from Donny and the men he's working with in Emily's cubby at preschool. Apparently, they paid the janitor to put it there. It had a note demanding money, along with photos of Emily and me that were taken while we were under police surveillance. They threatened to kill both me and Emily if I don't get them a hundred thousand dollars by ten tonight."

Jesus Christ! Son of a bitch!

Nate's rage shifted into overdrive. "Do the cops know?"

"Yes. I called them right away." Her voice quavered. "My brother is coming tonight to take me to stay at his place, but right now I'm just sitting in my house with an unmarked police car outside my door. I ... I don't want to sit here alone, waiting, and I thought maybe if you didn't mind... "

More than a little gratified that she had turned to him, he didn't hesitate. "Of course I don't mind. Head on up. I'll give you directions."

Nate tucked his wallet in the back pocket of his jeans and grabbed his coat and gloves. The drive to the ranch from Megan's house took about forty-five minutes, which meant she'd arrive at the gate in about fifteen minutes. He wanted to be there to ensure she wasn't followed. He walked to the gun safe, grabbed his SIG Sauer P226, slid it into his shoulder holster, then took out his shotgun and a case of double-aught buck shells.

If anyone came looking for trouble, he'd make damn sure they found it.

"Where the hell are you going?" His dad's voice came from behind him.

"Megan Hunter called." He quickly told his old man what Megan had told him. "She's afraid and doesn't want to be alone. She asked if she could bring her little girl up to look at the horses. I'm heading to the gate to meet her."

His dad frowned. "You know, a woman who's been through what she's been through—that's a lot for a man to take on."

"What's that supposed to mean?"

"It means she comes with baggage. I'm not judging her. I'm not saying she doesn't deserve a second chance. Hell, I followed her story every day in the paper for weeks. I even wrote a letter to the governor asking him to grant her a pardon. I think what happened to her was pretty goddamned awful. Even so, she's going to bring her troubles to your door."

Nate felt a spark of irritation. "None of this is her fault."

"That may be true, but think of it this way." His dad pointed to the shotgun. "You barely know her, and you're heading out to meet her loaded for bear."

Nate understood the point his old man was trying to make. "I can handle it."

His dad's frown deepened. "It's a damned stupid time for her to come up here anyway. Didn't she check the forecast? That storm they expected to dump thirty-six inches on the northwest part of the state took a detour and is headed straight for us."

Shit.

Nate glanced outside, saw a few fat flakes already falling. "It's too late now. She'll be at the gate in ten minutes."

CHAPTER 5

Megan turned off Squaw Pass Road onto County Road 270 and followed it as it twisted and turned through a forest of ponderosa pines and bare aspen, the high peaks hidden in a bank of storm clouds. Snow had begun to fall from a heavy, gray sky, forcing her to turn on the car's headlights and windshield wipers. She hoped the storm would die out. She didn't want to drive home in the dark in a blizzard.

According to the directions Nate had given her, the gate to the ranch was supposed to be about three miles up on the right. There was no one else on the road. The unmarked police car that had followed her up I-70 all the way to Evergreen Parkway had turned around and gone back to Denver. They were probably ticked with her, though not nearly as angry as Marc.

The guys assigned to watch her had called him the moment she'd pulled out of the driveway. He'd called a few minutes later and chewed her head off when she'd told him she was headed up to Nate's ranch.

"You're running again, Megan. This is an impulsive decision. You hardly know anything about this guy."

But Megan already knew what she needed to know about Nate.

She knew he'd already risked his life to protect her. She knew he wasn't behind the attack or the photos or the threats. She knew he wasn't a cop.

Of course, she hadn't told her brother that.

Marc trusted his fellow officers. He worked beside them every day. He didn't see the situation the way she did. Someone had followed her throughout the day and taken photos of her and Emily, and the police who'd been watching her hadn't even noticed. Either they didn't do their job very well, or maybe one of them was in on it.

She didn't trust them.

She glanced in the rearview mirror and saw Emily straining to see out the windows. "We're almost there, sweet pea."

And there it was—an archway constructed of big logs, a wooden sign bearing the words "Cimarron Ranch" hanging from the crossbeam.

Nate was waiting just outside the gate in a white Ford pickup. When he saw her, he climbed out of the cab, wearing a black cowboy hat, the collar of his shearling barn jacket turned up to keep out the snow, his hands in his pockets.

She stopped, rolled down the window, her pulse skipping when he smiled. "Hi."

"You found me." He bent down and looked in the window. "Hi, Emily. Are you ready to see some horses?"

"Uh-huh."

Megan glanced back in time to see her daughter nod. "I didn't know it was going to snow. I'm afraid we won't be able to stay very long. I want to make it back to town before the storm gets worse and the roads get slick."

"I think it might be too late for that." Nate tilted his head, glanced skyward. "Head on up the road. My dad is waiting for you at the house. I'll follow."

"Okay." Megan rolled up the window, the wipers squeaking as she accelerated up the dirt road, gravel crunching beneath the tires as she drove.

In her rearview mirror, she saw Nate climb back into his pickup. But rather than starting up the engine, he simply sat there. It took her a moment to realize that he was waiting to see whether she'd been followed.

And some of the tension she'd been carrying with her eased.

She'd driven for perhaps five minutes when she saw it—the ranch house. It was easily five times the size of her house. Built of stone and logs, it was a mix of Swiss chalet and western styles with a steeply sloped roof and high cathedral ceilings and windows. Several stone chimneys jutted from the roof, smoke curling against the gray sky. The front door was set back from a portico driveway accented by a colonnade of polished logs. Off to one side stood several very large outbuildings, including what looked like a horse barn, complete with several corrals. As the road curved around, she spotted the entrance to a multiple-car garage attached to the rear of the house

Ranch *house*? More like ranch mansion.

An older man—Nate's father?—stepped out of the house's front door and stood beneath the large portico. He waved to her, motioned for her to park near the front door. She pulled up, turned off the car, and opened the door.

"Welcome to the Cimarron, Megan. I'm Jack West, Nate's father." He extended a hand, gave hers a firm but friendly shake.

"It's a pleasure to meet you, Mr. West. Thanks for having us."

He smiled, and Megan saw a strong resemblance between father and son—the strong jaw, the eyes, the firm mouth. "I'm glad you beat the storm. Leave your keys in the ignition and take your little girl on inside where it's warm. I'll park the car. Nate will be right along."

Megan got Emily out of her car seat, watching from the doorway as Jack drove off in her car. She turned and went inside—and felt her jaw drop.

If she'd had a dream home, it might have looked like this. The living room had high timber ceilings, windows all around with views of the high peaks, and an enormous fireplace with a hearth and chimney made of rounded river stones. The floor was polished wood, the furniture made of wood and leather, paintings of Colorado landscapes framed on the walls. Everything from the lamps and lighting fixtures to the blinds and area rugs was tasteful.

No antlers. No dead animal heads. No animal skin rugs.

She took Emily to sit on a couch near the fire, basking in its warmth, while Emily watched the flames. Then on the mantel she saw it—what appeared to be a family portrait. She stood, took it down, and stared.

There was Nate standing between his mother and father in his marine dress uniform, a big smile on his handsome face. Megan had no idea how long ago the photo had been taken—sometime before Nate had been burned. He was beautiful, so handsome, the kind of man that made a woman go weak in the knees. Jack looked younger, too—fewer lines on his face, less gray in his hair. Nate's mother was a natural beauty. Nate had her cheekbones.

"That was Nate's graduation from Officer Candidate School." Jack's voice came from behind Megan, making her jump. "That was a proud day for me and my wife. Theresa's been gone these past five years, but I still miss her. She died suddenly. Aneurysm."

"I'm sorry for your loss." Megan put the photo back. "You made a beautiful family."

"Nate just pulled into the garage. He's heading over to the horse barn. I'll take you there." Jack leaned down. "You must be Emily, the girl who loves horses. Are you ready to see some real, live horses, sweetheart?"

And Emily smiled.

Nate saddled Buckwheat, the steadiest, most docile gelding he owned. "You ready for some excitement, boy?"

Buckwheat looked back at Nate through soft, dark eyes.

Nate led the horse through the stables to the indoor riding barn and tethered him to one of the posts. He heard Megan and Emily's voices coming from the stables and walked back to meet them. He found his dad standing at Baby Doe's stall, holding the pregnant mare's bridle, his pockets full of carrots, while Megan held Emily up, mother and daughter petting the animal's muzzle.

"Oh, her nose is so soft!" Megan's face lit up with a smile. "It's like velvet."

"It's called a muzzle." Nate came up beside her.

She looked over her at him, her smile growing brighter. "She's beautiful! I love her coloring."

Nate was struck again by how pretty Megan was—the all-American girl next door with a touch of pin-up sexy. But hers wasn't just a physical beauty. There was something about her—an inner light, an innocence, a vulnerability. Looking at her, he couldn't believe she'd survived so much brutality.

How strange it was to know so much about her. He knew about her childhood. He knew about her adoptive parents. He knew what had landed her in juvenile detention—and what had happened to her there. He knew what she'd done, how she'd finally landed in prison two months pregnant. And he knew how hard Marc Hunter had fought to protect her and Emily, almost losing his own life to save theirs.

The only trouble was that Megan didn't know Nate knew.

And that made him feel guilty as hell.

He patted the mare. "She's a palomino."

Megan's brows knit together in a frown, her cheeks pink from the cold, the bruise Donny had given her almost healed. "I thought she was a quarter horse."

"Quarter horse refers to her breed." Nate couldn't help but grin. "Palomino describes the color of her coat."

Megan smiled sheepishly. "I guess I don't know much about horses."

"Well, it's a good thing for you and little Miss Emily that we know plenty." Jack took a carrot from his pocket, broke off a piece and offered it to Emily. "Would you like to feed Baby Doe? Open your hand and let the carrot lie flat on your palm like this."

Emily held out her tiny hand and trustingly did as Nate's dad showed her, holding her hand open just beneath the mare's mouth.

Baby Doe took the carrot and crunched.

Emily squealed with delight.

"Can I try?" Megan looked as amazed and excited as her daughter.

"Sure." Jack handed Megan the rest of the first carrot. "Just keep your palm flat. There you go. That's right."

Megan and Emily laughed together as the mare fed from Megan's hand.

And Nate found himself sharing a smile with his dad.

They gave Megan and Emily a thorough tour of the stables, stopping to pet every horse along the way. They showed them the stalls where mares were kept when they were about to foal, the stalls where they were bred, and the cabinets where veterinary supplies were stored. Just for fun, Nate's dad opened a barrel of oats to show Emily what horses like to eat. While Emily played in the oats, Megan walked over to look at the tack. Unable to stop himself, Nate followed.

"Where are the stallions?"

"We have one. We keep Chinook in a separate stable."

She frowned. "Alone?"

"Yeah. He's got a powerful sex drive and will do anything to mate with a mare in season. He won't just kick down his stall and hers, he'll also attack the geldings and any horse that gets in his way. Not all stallions are as randy or aggressive as Chinook, but any stallion can be a real problem if not handled correctly."

Her eyes went wide. "Oh."

Nate led her toward the riding barn, his dad following with Emily, who skipped and ran and pretended to gallop. "Have you ever ridden a horse?"

Megan shook her head. "No."

Well, then he had a surprise for her.

When they entered the riding barn, she stopped. "Wow! This place is huge!"

"It's not as big as some, but it's enough for our needs. We're able to exercise the horses indoors when it's too cold or snowy outside." He walked over to Buckwheat, who waited patiently, and unhitched him. "This is Buckwheat. He's a big, old softie. I saddled him up so that you and Emily could go for a little ride."

"Ride? A horse?" Megan's eyes went wide, and she shook her head. "Oh, no. I don't think I could—"

"Sure you can. That's what people do with horses. I'll be right here to help you."

Nate's dad walked in, Emily in hand. "Are you ready to ride, Miss Emily?"

"Come here, Emily." Nate lifted Emily so that she could pet Buckwheat's muzzle. "Can you say hello to Buckwheat?"

"Hello, Buckwheat!" Emily's tiny voice rang out as she reached out to stroke the white star on the gelding's forehead. "You're a big horsie!"

If that wasn't the damned cutest thing Nate had ever seen…

"Do you want to ride him?"

Emily nodded.

Nate turned to Megan. "I'll help you into the saddle and adjust the stirrups, and then we'll settle Emily in front of you."

"I don't know the first thing about riding. Are… Are you sure this is safe?"

Nate smiled. "I'm sure. Buckwheat is gentle, and I'll have the reins."

"Okay." Megan walked over to the horse, looking as if she expected it to attack her.

And it hit Nate that so many people she ought to have been able to trust in her life had done just that. They'd neglected her, abused her, hurt her. He looked from her to the horse and realized that this would be good for Megan. The Cimarron had occasionally sold horses to an equine therapy program in Denver that helped abused children learn to trust again. There was no reason Buckwheat couldn't help Megan in that same way.

Nate walked up close behind her. "You have nothing to worry about. He's just a big teddy bear. See how calm he is?"

He took her left hand in his, stroked the gelding's flank with her palm, sparks of awareness darting through him the moment his skin touched hers.

Buckwheat gave a soft whicker, looked back at them, and nuzzled Nate's side.

Some of the tension seemed to leave Megan's body. "He likes you."

"He's looking for treats, aren't you, old boy?" Nate didn't have anything in his pocket this time. He released Megan's hand, checked the girth to make sure it hadn't come loose since he'd fastened it, then took a firm hold of the reins. "Grab the saddle, lift your left foot into the stirrup, then use the strength of your leg to lift yourself up and astride the horse. When you're seated, tuck your right foot in the other stirrup."

"Okay." She reached up and grasped the saddle, lifted her left foot until her toe caught the stirrup, then bounced on her right foot, struggling to mount.

"Let me help." Nate handed Buckwheat's reins to his dad and caught Megan around the waist, unable to keep from noticing the way her entire body tensed at the contact. "I'm just going to boost you. Give a little hop."

On her next bounce, he used her upward momentum to lift her into the saddle.

"Just settle in while I adjust the stirrups." He worked quickly, raising the left stirrup a few notches then doing the same to the right. "How do you feel?"

"Like I'm sitting miles off the ground on a very big animal that could kill me." She sat stiffly, as if she feared the gelding might buck if she moved.

"Buckwheat wouldn't hurt a flea." Nate took the reins back from his dad. "We'll just go for a walk so you can get used to this before we put Emily in the saddle. How does that sound?"

Megan gasped when the horse took its first steps.

"Easy, Megan. You're okay." Nate walked the perimeter of the riding barn, Buckwheat following meekly behind, all one thousand one hundred pounds of him.

They hadn't gone far when Nate heard Megan laugh. He looked behind him to see her smiling, her cheeks flushed with excitement. She seemed to have forgotten her fear—both her fear of the horse and the fear that had driven her here.

"See? No worries."

He stopped when he reached their starting point.

"Are you ready, little Miss Emily?" His dad walked over and lifted Emily into the saddle in front of Megan. "Megan, wrap one arm around Emily and use your free hand to hold onto the horn."

Emily bounced in the saddle. "Giddy-up, Buckwheat! Go!"

As obedient as Buckwheat was, he was above taking orders from a preschooler and remained defiantly still.

Fighting a chuckle, Nate let Megan get settled. "Ready?"

She nodded.

Nate started off again, sharing a smile with his dad at Emily's delighted squeal. The old man might have had reservations about the idea of Megan's coming here, but he'd sure gotten into the spirit of the thing—lured, no doubt, by an adorable four-year-old with big blue eyes. He watched while Nate led the gelding around the barn once, twice, clearly as gratified by Emily's happy chatter and the smile on Megan's face as Nate was.

"How old were you when you started riding?" Megan asked as they neared the end of their third lap.

"I don't remember *not* riding, so I must have been one or two." He glanced up to find Megan watching him.

"How long have you lived here?"

"My great-grandfather bought this spread, passed it down to my grandfather. Now it belongs to my dad. I've always lived here. My parents rebuilt the main house when I was in high school. I spent most of the past decade going wherever Uncle Sam sent me, but this is home."

"It must be wonderful to have such deep roots." There was a hint of longing in Megan's voice.

Nate halted Buckwheat.

His dad stepped forward. "Come on down, Miss Emily. Was that fun?"

Emily nodded, a big smile on her face.

"Your turn, Megan." Nate scratched Buckwheat's withers. "Just hold tight to the saddle or Buckwheat's mane, lift your right leg over, and lower yourself to the ground."

Megan nibbled her lower lip, looking down at the ground. "If I fall…"

"If you fall, I'll be right here to catch you." Nate watched as Megan grasped the pommel, lifted her right leg over the gelding's rump, and lowered herself toward the ground.

She'd almost made it when she lost her balance and began to fall backward, her left foot stuck in the stirrup.

He dropped the reins, caught her around the waist with his arm, and drew her back against his chest. He tried not to notice how his pulse ratcheted up the moment he touched her or how good she smelled or how sweet she felt in his arms, her body soft and feminine with curves in all the right places. "I've got you."

She turned in his arms and looked up at him through startled eyes. "Thank you."

And he knew she felt it too—that jolt of awareness, attraction.

For a moment, neither of them spoke or moved.

From somewhere nearby, Nate's dad cleared his throat. "Why don't you three head back to the house while I settle Buckwheat in his stall?"

Megan pulled away, reached for Emily's hand. "Thanks so much for this. I suppose we should be going before it gets too late or the roads get bad."

Nate walked to one of the side doors, opened it, and looked outside. Snow was falling thick and fast, the wind blowing hard, a good six inches already accumulated on the ground. He couldn't even see the house. "It's too late for that. It looks like you and Emily are our guests for the night."

Megan let out a sigh. "Marc is going to be ticked."

CHAPTER 6

Marc *was* ticked. "I knew you were going to get stuck up there. You barely know this guy. Are you involved with him?"

"No!" Megan felt her cheeks grow warm.

She wasn't involved with Nate, but she *was* attracted to him. Or at least she thought she was. When he'd come up behind her, closed his hand over hers, and guided her fingers over the horse's soft coat, she hadn't felt sickened by his touch. Instead she'd felt an unfamiliar heat shimmer through her that had made it hard to breathe. And when she'd lost her balance getting off the horse, the shock of finding herself in his arms, his body warm and muscular against hers, had made her mind go blank.

"You sure about that?"

"I just came here so Emily could see the horses. Being surrounded by cops … I needed to get away. I had no idea we were going to get hit with a blizzard."

And it was definitely a blizzard, the wind so strong that Megan had had to carry Emily, Nate guiding her from the stables to the house through near whiteout conditions, his arm around her shoulders.

"Do you trust him and his father around Emily?"

Megan glanced toward the kitchen, where Emily sat like a princess with a mug of hot cocoa and marshmallows, two big men seeing to her every whim.

"Yes. My pervert radar is pretty finely tuned, you know. I'm not catching any hinky vibes." Megan took a deep breath and said what she needed to say, something she'd needed to say for a while now. "I know I've made a lot of mistakes, but I'm not the same person I was ten years ago or even four years ago. You need to trust me, Marc."

For a moment Marc said nothing.

"You're right." The anger was gone from his voice. "I care about what happens to you. I don't want to see you hurt again."

"I know. You've always been there for me."

"No, not always." A heavy silence. "Well, I suppose you're safer up there than you would be down here. We're going through with the money drop tonight despite the storm. I have no idea if the bastards will show up. I guess we'll see."

Megan felt a hitch of fear in her stomach to think Marc and others would be out in the storm and in danger tonight. "Please be careful. I don't want you or anyone else to get hurt."

"Hey, we do this for a living, remember? I'll let you know how it goes."

"Thanks, Marc. I love you."

"Love you, too, sis."

Megan ended the call and walked back to the kitchen to find Emily with a cocoa mustache and a handful of extra marshmallows.

Nate looked up as she approached. "Everything okay?"

"Yeah." But Megan could tell he didn't believe her. "They're going to drop off the money tonight and see if anyone shows up to take it."

Jack stood, reached for a red-and-white checked apron that hung over the back of a nearby chair. "Nate has filled me in on what's happening, so here's my unsolicited advice. You're safe and warm up here, and there's nothing you can do about what happens in Denver tonight. So try to sit back, relax, and get ready to enjoy a pot of Cimarron Ranch Chili made by the expert. It's a life-changing experience."

Megan couldn't help but smile at this smug declaration. "Can I help?"

"No!" Jack shook his head. "You all get the hell out of my kitchen."

Nate shook his head, but the affection he felt for his father was plain to see. "Let me show you the house and get the two of you settled."

He led Megan around the main floor. In the center were the great room, formal dining room, and the kitchen, which she had already seen. On the far side of the kitchen were a walk-in pantry, a wine cellar, a bathroom, a laundry room, and the five-car heated garage. On the far side of the great room were Jack's office, three more bathrooms, an exercise room with a sauna, and a home theater with its own fireplace and an enormous flat-screen TV.

Upstairs, there were five bedrooms, each with its own television, bathroom and fireplace, and a library, which also had a fireplace and floor-to-ceiling windows that looked out toward the mountains. With the sun shining, the view would be staggering. As it was, all Megan could see was blowing snow.

"This is beautiful." Megan had seen wealth before. Her adoptive parents were relatively wealthy, and their friends had been wealthy. But never had she seen anything to equal the comfort and beauty of the Cimarron, glass and stone and wood tastefully joining the interior of the house to the landscape outside.

"It's a bit much for two people, but it's home." Nate led her to a bedroom with a big four poster bed covered with a blue and green quilt and matching shams. "Why don't we put you in here? Do you want to share a bed with Emily, or would you rather have a room to yourself?"

"Oh, we can definitely share a bed. I don't want to make any more trouble for you than I already have."

Nate reached up, brushed his thumb down her cheek, leaving a trail of heat on her skin. "You haven't made trouble for us, so put that idea out of your head."

For the span of a heartbeat, maybe two, she found herself looking up at him, lost in the warmth of his blue eyes.

"Th-thank you." Then she remembered. "I was planning to stay at Marc's tonight, so I packed suitcases. I need to get them from the trunk of the car."

"I'll get them. You just make yourself at home."

Home.

Megan sat on the bed and looked out the window at the swirling storm. And for the first time since Donny had forced his way back into her life, she felt ... *safe.*

Nate turned up the lights as the credits rolled on *Beauty and the Beast*, a movie he hadn't seen since... well, ever. He looked over to find Emily asleep on her mother's lap, looking sweet as candy in fuzzy pink pajamas, her tiny body limp. Megan held her daughter, stroking Emily's hair, a soft smile on her face. Out of nowhere, the photos from the Denver Independent article came back to him.

His urge to shelter and protect ratcheted up another notch. "Do you want me to carry her upstairs?"

Megan didn't look thrilled by the idea. She clearly trusted very few people with her little girl. Nate couldn't blame her for that. "It's pretty far, isn't it?"

"I promise I won't drop her."

Megan stood, shifting Emily into Nate's arms.

Emily's eyes opened, and she looked up at him from beneath heavy eyelids. She reached with one tiny hand, touched the scarred side of his face. Little blond brows furrowed, Emily's sleepy eyes filling with a child's sympathy. "Owie."

Her eyes drifted shut again, her hand curling beneath her chin as she snuggled against Nate's shoulder.

Blindsided by the child's simple gesture, her innocent compassion, Nate's throat went tight, a hitch behind his breastbone where his heart was supposed to be.

Get a grip, Marine.

He carried her down the hall, up the stairs, and into the guestroom, where his dad had a warm fire already burning. He waited while Megan pulled back the covers, then laid Emily gently on the bed, watching as Megan drew the blankets and quilt up to her daughter's chin, the moment satisfying something deep inside him.

He spoke quietly. "My dad and I usually end the day talking around the fire. You're more than welcome to join us."

Megan bent down to plant a kiss on Emily's forehead then stood and smiled at him in a way that made his pulse kick up a notch. "I'd like that."

She followed him downstairs, where they found his dad, tumbler of scotch in one hand, cell phone in the other. He was sending a text message, probably discussing his plans for tomorrow with Chuck, the foreman who'd been with the ranch as long as Nate could remember. They would need to drive hay out to the cattle every day now until the snow melted enough for the cows to forage again.

His dad looked up. "Is that adorable baby girl of yours tucked in?"

"Yes, she is." Megan sat across from him.

Nate reached for the bottle of Aberfeldy and a tumbler, poured himself a drink, truly needing it. "Want some scotch or a glass of wine?"

"I don't drink." She smiled almost apologetically. "But I wouldn't mind some of your hot chocolate."

"You got it." Nate set his drink aside and stood, but his old man stopped him.

"Sit down. I'll get it." His dad tossed back the rest of his scotch, tucked his cell phone in his pocket. "I make it from scratch, you know—milk, cocoa, sugar, touch of vanilla. None of that powdered shit."

"Thank you." Megan's lips twitched as she watched the old man walk away, a glint of laughter in her eyes. She met Nate's gaze. "Your father is a real character."

"He fought with the Army Rangers in Vietnam. I've always had a world of respect for him." Nate took a drink. "The past few years have been hard on him. He misses my mom. She died five years ago."

Megan's gaze shifted up to the family photo on the mantel. "He told me. I'm sorry for your loss."

Nate was surprised the old man had mentioned his mother to Megan. He didn't often speak of his grief. "I was downrange when it happened."

She got a puzzled look on her face.

Quit speaking in military jargon, jarhead.

"I was deployed in Afghanistan. I was deployed a lot."

"Is that why you're not married?" Megan's eyes went wide, and she began to babble. "Oh, God! I'm … I'm sorry. That's a personal question. I would think a handsome man like you … I mean … It's really none of my business."

"No, that's okay." Nate was both amused by her obvious embarrassment and moved by what she'd said. It had been a long damned time since anyone had called him handsome. "I was *almost* married once. I met Rachel in college. We reconnected when I was home on leave. I thought that was it. I proposed a couple years later. When I was wounded, it was just too much for her. She came to visit me about a week after I arrived at the Brooke Army Medical Center in San Antonio. I was drugged out of my mind. I thought she'd come to be with me, but she'd come to end it. She just couldn't handle it."

Nate watched the play of emotions in Megan's eyes—shock, sympathy, anger.

"What kind of woman breaks up with her fiancé when he's lying in a hospital bed? You were wounded serving your country. I'm sorry she hurt you, but if that's the kind of woman she is, I think she did you a favor."

"Maybe so." Her indignation touched Nate, made him smile.

"She should have been there the entire time, helping you in any way she could." The anger faded from Megan's face, her gaze filling with empathy. "It must have been very hard getting through that. There's nothing more painful than being abandoned by the people who are supposed to love you."

Even if Nate hadn't read the articles about Megan, he would've known she had personal experience with that kind of betrayal. It was there in her eyes.

Poor, sweet Megan.

And then Nate was no longer thinking about those dark days in the burn center. He was no longer thinking at all. He leaned in, trailed his thumb over the curve of Megan's cheek—and kissed her.

At the first brush of his lips against hers, she gasped. He wanted more, the shock of physical contact singing through him. He leaned closer, cupped her cheek, increased the pressure, teasing her lower lip with his tongue.

Oh, God, she tasted sweet!

She didn't pull away, but leaned closer, her lips going pliant.

"Hope you like marshmallows." The sound of the old man's voice interrupted them as he reappeared with a mug of cocoa, which he put on the coffee table. "Be careful. It's hot."

Nice timing, old man.

Megan jumped away from Nate as if scorched. Her cheeks bright pink, she turned her attention to the cocoa. "Thank you."

And for a moment, Nate's dad stood there, trying to pretend he hadn't seen the kiss. "Well, I'm going to hit the hay. You youngsters enjoy the fire. Tomorrow's going to be a busy day. Goodnight, Megan."

Megan looked up at him, mug of cocoa in hand. "Goodnight, Jack. And thanks for everything. Your chili really is fantastic."

"Damn straight it is—and you're welcome."

He turned and left the two of them alone.

Megan's heart was still racing as Jack disappeared up the stairs. Unable to look at Nate, she stared into the fire, gripping her mug of cocoa tightly between her palms, the ceramic hot against her skin.

Oh, God!

Nate had kissed her. He had *kissed* her. And she hadn't hated it. She hadn't felt repulsed. She hadn't pushed him away.

Had she enjoyed it?

The answer made her heart pound harder.

It had to be an accident. He'd surprised her, and they'd been interrupted. There hadn't been time for her revulsion to kick in.

Or maybe she really *had* enjoyed it.

"Megan." Nate took the mug from her hands and set it on the table. "Look at me, Megan."

Her pulse almost frantic, she did what he asked, the gentle understanding in his eyes taking away some of her panic. "Y-you kissed me."

"You noticed." He gave her a lopsided grin. "If we hadn't been interrupted, I would have kept kissing you."

And she felt it again—that strange flutter deep in her belly.

Almost unable to breathe, she watched as he slowly drew her hand to his lips and kissed it, his mouth lingering against her skin, heat shivering through her, his gaze never leaving hers. And then…

He seemed to be waiting for something, his gaze searching hers.

The moment passed.

He released her hand with a squeeze, gave her a smile. "You should drink your cocoa before it gets cold."

She exhaled in a long shudder, reached for her cocoa with trembling hands, and sipped, oblivious to the creamy, chocolate taste, thoughts and emotions so tangled inside her that she couldn't sort through them.

"Emily seems to have my dad wrapped around her pinky finger." Nate watched her, scotch tumbler in hand.

"Yeah." Megan struggled for words, a maelstrom raging inside her. Part of her wanted Nate to kiss her so she could see whether it had been real or just a fluke. Part of her wanted him to kiss her again just to *feel* it—the taste of his lips against hers, the heat of his tongue, the skipping of her own pulse. It had been… *intoxicating.* "You've both been so kind to her."

"She's a sweet little girl."

Megan couldn't help but smile, a sense of pride swelling inside her. Emily was the only part of her life unmarred by her past. "I think so, but then I'm pretty biased."

"Emily is lucky to have you for her mother."

Some part of Megan wanted to tell him the truth—that she'd been in prison during the first year of Emily's life, leaving her daughter in the care of a Mennonite foster family, that she'd had to fight like hell to straighten herself out so she could win custody of her daughter back again, that some part of her still wondered whether she was even fit to be a mother.

But she liked seeing herself the way Nate saw her.

And so she said nothing—and immediately felt a stab of guilt.

After all he'd done for her, didn't Nate deserve the truth?

Nate grinned. "She looks so much like you—your eyes, your nose, your smile. Were you blond as a little girl?"

Megan nodded. "Strawberry blond."

Nate's eyes narrowed. "So why aren't *you* married? I would think that a woman as pretty as you… "

The question took Megan by surprise, though it shouldn't have. Hadn't she asked him the same thing not ten minutes ago? He'd even parroted her words. "I… I'm not really into the whole dating thing."

She was giving Nate half truths again. It wasn't that she was uninterested in dating; she was terrified of it. Dating went together with sex, and she didn't like sex. She'd never enjoyed it, never liked having a man's hands on her. Maybe if her life had been different…

Except that tonight Nate had kissed her, and she *had* liked it.

"Maybe you just need to meet the right man." Something about the way Nate said it, something in his deep voice, made Megan's pulse spike again.

And she found herself wishing she could forget what had been done to her, what *she* had done, and just pretend that she was whole and unbroken.

The conversation drifted after that, Nate telling her about their herd and what they would have to do to keep the cattle fed and safe in deep snow—plowing the road so their trucks could get through, carrying hay out every day, watching for sick animals.

"That's a lot of work for two people."

He chuckled. "That's why we have a crew—a foreman and five hands. They stay in the bunkhouse and handle a lot of the heavy work now that my father is getting older. He manages the financial and logistical sides of the operation."

"What do you do?"

"Sometimes I help with the herd, but mostly I work with the horses—training them, overseeing the breeding program, helping the mares foal if they have trouble."

It was such a different life than the one Megan knew. "You're a real cowboy."

Nate grinned and tipped an imaginary cowboy hat. "Why, yes, ma'am, I reckon I am."

Megan laughed at his exaggerated western twang.

"Tell me about your job."

There wasn't much to tell—except that Megan was very lucky to *have* a job. Very few employers were willing to take a risk on someone with a prison record. "I'm a graphic artist with the city's recreation department."

"Is that what you've always wanted to do?"

She shook her head. "It's a job."

She didn't tell him she'd gotten her start working in the print shop in prison. She'd gotten an associate degree while she was on parole. Her salary wasn't great, but she'd paid off her house and car with part of her court settlement.

"Is there anything you really wanted to do?"

"I always dreamed of going to law school." For a time, it had been her life's dream to help young women like herself, to make sure that someone always listened to them so that what had happened to her wouldn't happen to anyone else. But with past felonies, she would almost certainly be denied admittance to the bar, even if she passed the bar exam with flying colors.

On the mantel, a clock chimed, drawing Megan's gaze.

Ten.

The money drop.

Worries she'd tried to set aside through the evening rushed back at her.

Please stay safe, Marc! Keep everyone safe.

Nate took her hand, gave it a squeeze. "Your brother knows what he's doing. He'll be all right. I just hope they get the bastards."

"So do I."

"How long has this Donny asshole been stalking you? Why did he choose you? Who is he anyway?"

"He's been stalking me for almost three years now." Megan would have given almost anything in that moment *not* to answer the second part of Nate's question, but she couldn't ignore him or lie. "He's... He's Emily's father."

CHAPTER 7

Donny Lee Thomas was Emily's father.

Working in the pre-dawn dark, Nate lowered the snowplow on the front of his Ford F-150, put the truck into gear and drove forward, punching through more than three feet of snow, the forcefulness of it only partly satisfying his need for aggression.

What kind of man terrorized and attacked the mother of his child, tried to rob her, threatened to harm his own daughter?

No, not a man. A monster.

A *man* would have done all he could to make certain both mother and child were safe. A *man* would have provided his share of financial support. A *man* would have been a father to his child, even if he and the child's mother weren't together and hated each other's guts.

Nate could not wrap his mind around the fact that a bastard as revolting and fucked up as Donny could be Emily's father. Nate had gotten a good look at him—rotten teeth, sallow, unhealthy skin, dark, greasy brown hair. There was no trace of him on that sweet little girl's face.

Haven't you always said it's more the dam than the sire that makes the foal?

And that was the other thing.

Nate couldn't stand the thought that this son of a bitch had gotten his hands on Megan. It wasn't jealousy he was feeling. Hell, he knew Megan wasn't a virgin—and it wasn't just the fact that she had a child that gave that away. Like everyone who'd read those articles in the Denver Independent, Nate knew *how* she'd lost her virginity. Nothing he'd ever read in a newspaper had sickened him more.

Oh, Megan!

He'd seen the shame on her face when she'd told him the truth about Donny. She hadn't been able to look him in the eye. But he didn't believe for one minute that she'd met Donny, gotten to know him, and decided he was something she wanted a piece of. Given Megan's past, it was far more likely that he'd taken advantage of her in some way or forced himself on her.

The thought had gnawed at Nate last night until he'd gotten up at almost two in the morning, gone down to his dad's office, found the file on Marc Hunter and read through the articles about Megan again. None of the stories had mentioned Donny, but Nate was pretty certain he'd pieced it together.

If Donny came any where near Megan again, Nate would rip him apart—balls, blood, and bones.

Of course, it wasn't just learning the truth about Donny that had kept Nate awake half the night. It was also the junk that hung about eight inches below his navel. How he could be so angry and so horny at the same time, he didn't know. He'd had to beat one out before he'd finally been able to sleep.

Kissing Megan had been such a *bad* idea. He hadn't planned it. He'd just done it. And now he was paying for it.

He probably owed the old man a thank you for barging in like that. Nate had been so caught up in the sweet taste of her that it was only *after* the kiss had ended that he'd realized he ought to have asked Megan how she felt about being kissed *before* locking lips with her. He'd given her a moment, trying to gauge her response but...

Had that been desire he'd seen in her eyes—or had it been fear?

He needed to know, because if it had been desire, he wanted to pick up where they'd left off. And if it had been fear?

It was time for someone to prove to Megan that not all men were thugs.

Are you sure you're the man for that job, West?

He remembered his dad's warning. Yeah, a single mother with a traumatic past was a lot to take on, but Nate understood a thing or two about scars. Megan was the first woman he'd met since he'd been burned who made him feel like a man. More than that, he cared about her. He'd been drawn to her from the first moment he'd seen her chopping vegetables in the community kitchen. He couldn't say why exactly, but *why* no longer mattered. It was just a fact. And he wasn't about to turn his back on the feeling inside him—or on her or her little girl.

By the time Nate reached the front gate, the sun was just beginning to rise in the east, its light hidden behind an overcast sky, heavy clouds to the northwest promising more snow. The entrance was blocked by a snow drift at least six feet deep and twenty feet wide, the gate's bars catching blowing snow, causing it to pile up.

Shit.

So much for making it to breakfast on time.

Megan cut up Emily's buttermilk pancakes, real maple syrup trickling down over the edges, the mingled scents coming from Jack's griddle making her mouth water—bacon, scrambled eggs, rising pancake batter. "Eat your scrambled eggs, first, okay, sweet pea? Then you can have your pancakes."

"Pancakes?" Jack turned to look at them, a grumpy frown on his face, spatula in hand, red checked apron covering his gray turtle neck and jeans. "Excuse me? I'll have you know these are flapjacks." He shifted his gaze to Emily. "Can you say flapjacks?"

"Fwap-jacks!" Emily smiled, pointing at Jack. "Fwap-jacks, because you're Jack."

Megan laughed at Emily's perfectly logical conclusion.

"That's right, sugar." Jack turned back to his griddle. "The girl's all of four years old, and she's already a damned genius."

Megan glanced at the clock—it was almost seven thirty. She'd called the office first thing this morning to tell them she'd be late only to get a recorded message telling her that all city offices were closed for the day because of the storm. That meant a three-day weekend—and no need to worry about being late or missing another day of work. It wasn't that she needed the money. She had more than a million dollars of settlement money in the bank that she hoped to pass on to Emily. She just didn't want to get fired, not when finding another job would be next to impossible.

She glanced at Nate's empty place at the table. Jack had told her Nate had gone out to plow the road leading to the highway and that he'd be back in time for breakfast. That had been an hour ago. She hoped Nate was okay—and that he wasn't skipping breakfast as a way of avoiding her.

The look on his face when she'd told him Donny was Emily's father had been one of shock and revulsion. She'd known what he was thinking: What had been wrong with her that she'd slept with a man like Donny Lee Thomas? She'd been grateful that he hadn't asked her questions, that he hadn't asked her to explain. The fact that Donny was Emily's father was something she tried hard every day to forget.

One thing was certain—Nate wouldn't kiss her again.

She sat at the place Jack had set for her and put her napkin on her lap, debating calling Marc to find out how things had gone last night, but afraid she'd wake him. He was probably still asleep after having been up most of the night. Deciding to wait, she gave in to her hunger and the delicious smells around her—and took her first bite.

She moaned. The pancakes melted in her mouth, all buttery and maple sweet. The last time she'd had real buttermilk pancakes made from scratch had been when she was living with Pastor John and Connie. Connie had cooked everything from scratch, Sunday morning breakfast a feast of pancakes or French toast, hash browns, eggs, and bacon, topped off with hot cocoa.

John and Connie were the closest thing she'd ever had to real parents. They'd given her a safe haven when she'd fled the police with Emily in her arms. Connie had died two years ago, John not that long after, as if he couldn't stand to be parted from his wife.

Megan missed them each and every day.

She licked syrup off her fork. "Jack, you are an amazing cook."

He glanced over at her for a moment before flipping the next batch of flapjacks. "They're mostly my wife's recipes. I didn't start cooking until after she passed on. I figured I needed to eat, and learning to cook the way she'd cooked would be a way of learning more about her and keeping a part of her here with us."

A hard lump formed in Megan's throat, making it hard for her swallow.

To be loved like that …

A door opened, and Megan heard footsteps coming from the garage. A few moments later, Nate appeared, his face red from the cold.

"Mornin'." He gave Megan a smile, ruffled Emily's hair. "Mornin', cutie. That looks really tasty."

At the warmth in his eyes, Megan felt an enormous knot of tension melt away inside her. "Good morning."

Emily tilted her head back and looked straight up at him, clutching her fork in one sticky hand. "Jack made fwapjacks."

"That's good, because I'm hungry." He looked over at his dad. "We've got at least thirty-six inches out there."

Megan groaned inwardly, certain the drive home would be a nightmare.

Jack nodded. "Chuck got the trucks loaded?"

"Yeah. He was heading out as I was coming in." Nate walked toward the counter. "Got any coffee? These womenfolk might do alright with hot cocoa in the morning, but a man's got to have himself a cup of strong coffee."

Nate glanced over at Megan, gave her a wink, a look in his eyes that told her he might just kiss her again after all.

Her pulse skipped.

It took her a moment to realize her cell phone was buzzing. She pulled it out of her pocket, looked at the caller ID.

Marc.

N ate poured himself a mug of coffee, watching as Megan rose from her chair and walked out of the kitchen, cell phone to her ear. He exchanged a glance with his dad and knew he and his old man were hoping the same thing—that Donny Lee Thomas and his crew had woken up inside a jail cell this morning. Hell, Nate wouldn't mind if Donny hadn't woken up at all. That would be fine, too.

Nate sat, put his napkin in his lap, plunged his fork through a stack of three flapjacks, and dragged them onto his plate. "Have you ever had flapjacks as yummy as these ones?"

Emily looked up at him and shook her head, her big blue eyes filled with a child's honesty, her mouth full, both her lips and her fingers sticky.

"I'm glad you like them." Nate poured syrup on his pancakes, added bacon and eggs to his plate, and dug in, his thoughts with Megan in the next room.

"Forecast is calling for another foot tonight."

Nate washed down a bite of eggs with a gulp of coffee, the conversation feeling like small talk, a way of filling the silence as he waited for Megan's news. "I believe it. There's a heavy bank of storm clouds moving in from the northwest."

"Last time we got this much snow in November, we were buried through spring." Nate's dad sat across from him, mug of coffee in one hand, breakfast plate in the other. "It looks like we're in for a long winter."

Megan walked into the kitchen, cell phone still in hand, an unreadable expression on her face. She sat, spread her napkin on her lap, gave them a tight smile. "That was Marc. He's safe. No one was hurt—thank goodness! They got three men—the guys who were in the car that night. They were still driving the Lincoln Continental."

"Well that's good news." His tax dollars at work. "What about Donny?"

Megan shook her head, her gaze downcast, the tension inside her palpable.

"Let's hope the other goons rat him out." Nate's dad poured syrup over his flapjacks.

"Marc says that's what they're hoping, too." Her voice was tightly controlled. "I had hoped he'd be in custody before I got back to Denver today."

Nate jabbed his fork into another bite of flapjacks. "I hate to break it to you, but you're not going back to Denver today."

She lifted her gaze to his. "I'm... I'm not?"

"There's three feet of snow out there with more on the way. In some places, the wind has piled the snow up in six-foot drifts. Besides, both I-25 and I-70 are closed."

Nate's dad backed him up. "You'd best stay here until the snow stops and they get the roads cleared. There's no sense in taking chances."

Megan looked back and forth between Nate and his dad. "I don't want to impose."

"You're not imposing, Megan. I invited you up here, remember?" Nate covered her hand with his, gave it a squeeze.

She returned the squeeze. "Thanks."

"I got plans to put the both of you to work." Nate's dad fixed a sharp gaze on Emily, who was now nibbling on her bacon. "You think you can help Nate with the horses today, Miss Emily?"

Emily nodded, her eyes going wide. "Can I see Buckwheat?"

Nate shared a smile with Megan. "You bet."

Megan watched while Nate rode around the barn on Buckwheat with Emily in the saddle in front of him, a helmet on her head, a big smile on her face. Wearing that black cowboy hat, his fleece barn jacket, and leather work gloves, he looked like he'd ridden out of a Western movie—all man and leather and horse.

"Make him trot now."

Emily made a clucking sound with her tongue, squeezing the horse with her little legs. The gelding responded immediately by going faster, Emily's laughter filling the small arena.

"Tell him he's a good boy when he does what you want him to do."

"Good boy, Buckwheat!" Emily patted the horse's neck. "You're a good horsie."

Around and around the barn they rode. Nate managed the reins with one hand, his right arm wrapped around Emily, his confidence and care with her putting Megan at ease. This was Emily's reward for "helping" Nate lead the horses out to pasture where they were given fresh hay and warmed, ice-free water. Emily was in paradise.

"Now let's try loping him." Nate made a little kissing sound, shifted one foot, and the horse went faster.

Emily squealed.

Megan couldn't help but laugh, too, the sight of Emily's happiness smoothing the rough edges off her nerves. She needed to quit worrying. Donny had no idea where she was, and even if he did, he wouldn't be able to come after her. If she couldn't make it to Denver, he wouldn't be able to make it out to the Cimarron.

This was a chance for her to relax. Donny's accomplices—or at least some of them—were behind bars. Marc was safe. She and Emily were safe. She had a three-day weekend and was staying in one of the most beautiful homes in the state, warm and toasty high in the Rockies, with great food and hosts who were going out of their way to make her and Emily feel safe and welcome.

It was like a surprise vacation—with the added element of a heartbreakingly brave and handsome combat veteran who seemed to be attracted to her and who knew how to make her daughter laugh.

The door behind her opened with a blast of frigid air, and Jack walked up beside her. He watched for a moment, chuckling. "It wasn't too long ago that Nathaniel was that age. We started him riding as soon as he could walk. By the time he was Emily's age, he was riding by himself."

Megan stared at Jack, amazed. "Weren't you afraid he'd fall or get bucked off?"

Jack smiled. "Theresa and I stayed close by, and we only put him on horses we trusted. What was that old gelding's name? Cider. That's right. Old Cider. Beautiful horse."

As Nate and Emily drew near, Nate brought Buckwheat to a walk. "Say, 'Whoa,' and draw back gently on the reins."

"Whoa!" said Emily, her hands guided by Nate's.

Buckwheat drew to a halt with a snort.

"Alright, little Miss Emily, old Jack will help you down." Jack reached up.

Nate handed Emily to his father, dismounted, turned to Megan. "Your turn."

Megan took a step back. "That's fine. I don't need to ride again."

Nate raised an eyebrow. "You enjoyed it last time."

She had. She'd felt a sense of exhilaration sitting on the horse—after she'd gotten over being terrified. But now the idea made her nervous again. Just because it had gone well once didn't mean she wouldn't get bucked off this time.

But, not to be outdone by a preschooler, she gave in. "Okay, but you stay right here."

Nate grinned. "Hey, I'm not going anywhere."

Megan grasped the saddle, put her foot in the stirrup and with a boost from Nate, pulled herself astride the enormous animal. She waited while Nate took off his gloves and adjusted the stirrups, Buckwheat standing patient and still beneath her. She reached up, patted his neck, the dark hair of his mane coarse against her fingers.

"Here you go." Nate handed her the reins.

She stared at them, horrified to find them in her own hands. She handed them back to him. "Oh, no! You should keep them."

He frowned, caught her fingers with his, his hands so much bigger than hers—and much warmer. "Your hands are freezing. Wear these."

He retrieved the leather gloves he'd tucked under one arm and held the reins while she slid the gloves on. They were too big for her, but inside they were soft and warm from his body heat. "Thanks."

"Now, you're going to take the reins, and I'm going to teach you how to walk and trot the horse." He handed the reins back to her.

She took them, feeling suddenly very high off the ground. "Wh-what if he bucks me off or takes off running?"

Nate stroked the gelding's neck, looking up at her from beneath the brim of his cowboy hat. "There are good horses that would never harm their riders, and there are bad-tempered horses that bite and kick and won't settle down. Buckwheat's one of the good ones. Trust him, Megan."

Megan drew a deep breath, her heart hammering. "Okay. What do I do?"

"First, relax. A horse can tell when a rider is afraid. You've got nothing in the world to be afraid of. I'm here. My dad is here. That's almost a century of riding experience right here in this barn."

Megan drew another deep breath and another, willing herself to relax.

Nate tugged on the stirrup. "Sit up straight in the saddle so that your shoulder, hip, and foot are aligned. Hold the reins loosely so you're not pulling on them."

She did what Nate said, barely able to breathe, unable to believe she was about to ride a horse by herself.

"Perfect." He smiled up at her. "Now, to make him walk, cluck and give a light squeeze with your heels."

Megan hesitated. "How will you catch me if I fall?"

"You won't fall.

Megan gave a cluck, squeezed the horse's sides with her heels—and Buckwheat began to walk. Perhaps because the riding arena was small and he was used to being ridden here, Buckwheat didn't seem to need her to tell him where to go, his big, hard body graceful beneath her as he moved, his delicate ears twitching, turning from Megan toward the sound of Emily's happy chatter and then back again.

Soon, she reached the spot where Nate, Emily, and Jack stood watching her.

"Do you see your pretty mommy, Emily?" Nate asked, smiling up at Megan. "What's she doing?"

Megan felt her cheeks go warm.

"She's riding Buckwheat." Emily answered.

"That's right—and she's doing just fine."

Twice more Megan walked the horse around the arena.

"Now you're going to make him trot. Ready?"

Megan nodded, feeling braver.

"Just give a steady squeeze with your legs."

She squeezed Buckwheat's broad sides—and he shifted his gait, moving into a trot.

"Perfect," Nate called to her. "Let your hips and bottom absorb the motion."

She tried doing what Nate asked, searching for a way to settle into the horse's motions, and felt some of the jarring ease away. And it struck Megan that Buckwheat wasn't just some big, scary, dangerous animal. He was truly listening, paying attention to their voices, to the subtlest movements of her body, wanting to please her.

She patted him as Emily had done, spoke softly to him. "What a beautiful horse you are, Buckwheat."

Buckwheat's ears turned toward her as she spoke, and he gave a snort.

She found herself laughing, her fear gone, that sense of wild exhilaration returning. She rode around the barn four times, following Nate's instructions to slow Buckwheat to a walk and then draw him to a halt.

Nate took the reins. "How was that?"

Megan couldn't stop smiling. "Can I do it again?"

Jack shook his head. "Like mother, like daughter."

CHAPTER 8

Nate was in over his head where Megan was concerned—and he didn't give a damn. Watching joy replace the fear on her face had filled him with a kind of happiness he hadn't known in ages. She had trusted Buckwheat, which meant she had trusted him.

If she could learn to trust again in small ways...

Where are you headed with this, West?

He had no idea.

Did he want to sleep with her? Hell, yeah, he did. One kiss had set him on fire. But there was more to what he felt for her than sexual desire. She made him feel alive again, and he was pretty certain he was good for her, too. For now, that was enough.

But taking time out for Emily and Megan's riding "lessons" had put Nate behind. He ate a quick lunch—the old man made grilled cheese sandwiches and cream of tomato soup—and spent the afternoon mucking out the stables and making sure the horses had fresh hay and clean water waiting for them. Then he saddled and rode Chinook, who got ornery if he didn't get enough exercise. By the time he'd groomed the stallion and settled him and the other horses in their stalls for the night, snow was falling again, thick and fast. Nate climbed into his truck and plowed the road down to the gate once more, turning toward home just as darkness began to fall, his mind on a hot shower, a warm meal—and Megan.

He parked the truck in the garage, stopping in the mud room to take off his winter gear before heading indoors. He found his dad in the kitchen peeling potatoes, the house filled with the scents of roasting chicken, onion, sage, and…

"Chocolate cake?" Nate's mouth watered, and he clapped his dad on the shoulder. "You're going all out."

His dad sliced a peeled potato, dropped it in a pot of boiling water. "I know from experience that females need a certain amount of chocolate. We have two of them in the house. I don't want them growing restless."

Nate grinned. "Emily asked you to bake it, didn't she?"

His dad frowned, but there was a glint of humor in his eyes. "What are you implying?"

"I know who runs this household, and she's four."

"I'm not the only man in this house who's whipped." His dad glanced over at him through narrowed eyes. "I know what you were doing today, trying to help Megan trust you."

Had it been that obvious? "So what if I was?"

"It's going to take more than a few minutes in the saddle to heal the kind of hurt that girl carries inside her."

"I know that."

"Good—and good idea, by the way." His dad looked over at him, a moment of understanding in his eyes before he frowned. "Go take a shower. You smell like horse shit."

Chuckling, Nate walked out of the kitchen but was stopped by a squeal coming from the backyard. He walked over to the glass doors and spotted Megan and Emily sledding down the little hill behind the house. Their cheeks were red with the cold, bright smiles on their faces as they trudged to the top of the hill again, dragging Nate's old sled behind them. Megan settled onto the sled, drew Emily onto her lap—and they were off again, zooming down the hill, Emily laughing all the way.

The old man is right. You're whipped, West. You're both whipped.

Oddly, the thought put a smile on Nate's face.

Megan listened while Nate read Emily a bedtime story, her daughter's eyelids heavy, Emily's freshly washed hair smelling sweetly of baby shampoo. It had been a thrilling day for her—horses in the morning and sledding in the afternoon. Between the excitement and the cold mountain air, she was completely frazzled. Before Nate finished the story, she had fallen sound asleep.

Megan drew up the covers, pressed a kiss against her daughter's forehead. She turned to Nate, spoke in a whisper. "Thank you."

Nate whispered back, a half-grin on his face. "My pleasure."

He motioned with a jerk of his head toward the door, and Megan followed, thinking they were going to join Jack around the fire. But when they got downstairs, Jack wasn't there. And her pulse picked up, remembering what had happened last night when Jack had left them alone.

Nate walked over to the fireplace, added a few pieces of wood to the blaze, then poured himself a drink. "Can I make you some hot cocoa?"

Megan sat on the sofa, tucking her feet beneath her, trying not to feel nervous—or excited. "Oh, no, thank you. If I have any more chocolate, I'll be awake all night."

He came and sat down beside her. "It looked like you and Emily had fun with my old sled today."

SKIN DEEP   91

Nate had watched them? The idea warmed her.

"It was Emily's first time sledding." And the first time Megan had gone sledding in…

She couldn't remember how long.

"Really?" Nate's eyebrows went up. "I'm glad my dad kept that old thing."

"That was your sled?" Megan found herself smiling, an image of Nate as a little boy sliding down that same hill in her mind.

"Oh, yeah."

She listened while Nate told her how he'd once tied the sled to his horse's saddle so that the horse could pull him through the snow.

"I gave him a little cluck, and he started off. The rope wasn't very long, and one of his hooves hit the sled. That spooked him. Old Cider bucked and ran, dragging me behind him." Nate grinned, a faraway kind of smile. "It probably lasted less than a minute, but it seemed like an eternity to eight-year-old me. My old man heard the commotion and came running out. He managed to get hold of Cider's bridle. I scrambled off the sled, untied the rope, and helped my dad get Cider back in his stall."

"Did you get into trouble?"

"Oh, hell, yeah." Nate chuckled. "My dad asked me to help him groom Cider. While I helped brush him down, my dad showed me exactly how afraid Cider had been, pointing out how the horse was still shivering, and skittish. 'Think of all the things Cider has done for you,' my dad said. 'He trusts you, and today you betrayed that trust.' I felt lower than dirt."

Megan couldn't help but smile. "It must have been so wonderful to grow up with Jack as your father. He's so kind to Emily. She just adores him."

"He adores her, too. She's a special little girl."

"Sometimes I wonder how I ended up with her, why she came to me." Megan had only ever admitted this to Marc and Sophie. She was surprised to find herself telling Nate and wished for a moment that she could take the words back. They cut far too close to the truth about her.

Nate's gaze met Megan's, his left hand sliding over hers, his fingers warm as they twined with hers. "I guess the head stork felt she needed a special mother to raise her."

Megan forced a smile onto her face, looked away, a clammy sense of guilt sliding through her even as some part of her welcomed his touch. She needed to tell him the truth. He deserved to know.

Oh, but she didn't want to tell him! She liked this version of herself better, the version she saw reflected in his eyes—a good mother, a woman he respected, a woman without a criminal record, without blood on her hands. The moment she told him the truth, that woman would cease to exist. His attraction to her would vanish. He would draw his hand away, quit touching her. And although she didn't know him well, he was a good man. She cared what he thought of her. To lose his respect…

"What is it?" There was concern in his voice, his fingers tightening reassuringly around hers. "What's wrong?"

It was on the tip of her tongue to make some excuse, but the words wouldn't come. If she let this go any further, he would feel misled.

This is the price you pay. It's the price you'll always pay.

There really was no such thing as starting over.

She drew her hand away, her mouth suddenly dry. "Nate, I… I'm not the woman you think I am."

Oh, God! How was she going to do this?

She willed herself to meet his gaze. "When I was younger, I did things I shouldn't have done. I've served time in prison for using drugs, and I... I killed a man."

Nate reached out, stroked her cheek with his thumb. "I know, Megan. I know."

Megan stared at him, his words and his actions making no sense to her. "What... ?"

"I know you spent time in juvenile detention for shoplifting, and I know what happened to you there. I know about the man you shot and killed, and I know why you did it. I know your brother took the fall and spent six years of a life sentence in prison, while you struggled with heroin addiction on the streets. I know you were sent to prison on drug charges when you were two months pregnant with Emily, and I know what happened that set matters straight—why you disappeared with Emily, how your brother escaped and came after you, how the courts finally gave you both your freedom.

"I know it all, Megan, and I think no less of you for it."

Megan saw Nate's mouth moving, but couldn't hear him, her heart pounding so hard that it drowned out everything else. "Reverend Marshall told you."

"No, Megan. I read about it in the articles that ran in the Denver Independent. There was that series—"

She found herself on her feet, her face burning with rage and humiliation. "You googled me! You pried—"

"No, I didn't." He stood, took a step toward her.

"Oh, God!" She turned her back on him, stared down unseeing at the fire. "You went behind my back and—"

"That's *not* what happened." Nate was standing behind her now, his big hands coming to rest on her shoulders. "My dad is a news geek. He kept a folder from when your brother escaped from prison. He clipped all the articles—the ones about Marc, the ones about you. He recognized Marc's name and showed me the folder a few hours before you called yesterday."

"Jack knows, too?" Something inside her seemed to wither at this news, and she pulled away from Nate, tears pricking her eyes, her stomach in knots.

"He wrote letters to the governor asking him to grant you a pardon."

These last words broke through the adrenaline haze in Megan's mind. She turned to face Nate. "He... he did?"

"Yeah." Nate wiped a tear off her cheek with his thumb. "Megan, we've both known the whole story since before you came up here."

"You didn't say anything." They hadn't treated her strangely, either, showing her only courtesy and kindness, as if her past didn't matter to them, as if they didn't hold it against her.

"Why should I? Asking you about it would only dredge up painful memories. You don't owe me any explanations. Who you were then is not who you are now, and I'm interested in the woman you are today."

Stunned by Nate's response, Megan could do nothing but stare up at him.

Nate sat, empty tumbler in hand, listening while Megan spoke. He hadn't asked her to explain anything, but she seemed to need to talk about it now that her past was out in the open. What she had to say wasn't easy to hear.

"I was a virgin the first time. It hurt so bad. They came almost every night after that. There were four of them, and they took turns, using their radios to keep track of the other guards, covering for one another. One of them would come in, force me onto my back and rip down my pants. He would ... rape me, and then the next one would come in and do the same. They gave us candy bars, as if chocolate could somehow make up for what they'd done. They always wore condoms. No babies, no evidence, they said."

Rage thrummed inside Nate's chest. He knew all of this, of course. He'd read it in the paper. Megan had run away from her adoptive parents, had been arrested for trying to steal a warm coat, and had been placed in juvenile detention, where she, like the other girls in her unit, had been raped almost every day for six months. It had been hard enough to stomach when he'd read the words on newsprint—adult men in a position of trust and authority taking advantage of young girls who were under their power, girls with nowhere to run and no one to turn to, girls whose lives were already a mess. But seeing the torment on Megan's pretty face, watching the way she seemed to fold up right before his eyes, her arms wrapped tightly around her middle as if she feared her body might come apart...

He wanted to slam his fist through the wall. He wanted to hunt down the bastards who'd done this to her, ram their dicks down their throats, and put a bullet between their eyes. Too bad all but one of them were already dead, because they'd gotten off easy. The most he could do to them now was piss on their graves. As for the son of a bitch who was still alive—he was serving a life sentence for rape and murder and would spend the rest of his life in a wheelchair, impotent and incontinent, thanks to a bullet from Marc Hunter's gun.

That, at least, felt like justice.

Nate fought to keep his voice calm. "You must have felt so alone and afraid."

She nodded, her body trembling now. "I reported them. I got an infection and told the doctor everything. The rapes stopped, but no one believed us."

Nate had read how the guards had sabotaged the investigation, claiming that the girls had seduced them to win favors and privileges. The investigators had bought into their bullshit. And when Megan had been released, she'd been left to deal with the aftermath alone because the Rawlingses, her adoptive parents, didn't want her back.

Nate wouldn't mind having a few minutes alone with the Rawlingses. They'd adopted Megan at the age of four after her mother was sent to prison for drunk driving and vehicular assault. They'd refused to adopt 10-year-old Marc, tearing brother and sister apart. They'd given Megan too little love and too many beatings with a belt. But Hunter hadn't forgotten the little sister he'd lost, and after a few tours of duty in Iraq, he'd left the army and gone in search of her—only to find her strung out on heroin and living on the streets.

"I have to give your brother credit for tracking you down the way he did." Nate stood, took a throw off a nearby chair, and wrapped it around Megan's shoulders.

Megan's lips curved into a hint of a smile. "When he found me, it was one of the happiest days of my life. He put me in rehab and moved me into his house. I got clean, got on my feet again. I went to work on my GED. I had plans to go to college. I felt so full of hope, so certain that I'd turned my life around. I was wrong."

Her smiled faded. "Sometimes I wish he *hadn't* found me—for his sake."

Nate was certain she didn't mean that, and so he let it pass. "Why didn't you tell him what had happened to you? Why didn't you tell him about the guards?"

Megan shrugged as if the answer was obvious. "No one believed me—the cops who investigated it, the people who were supposed to be my parents. Marc was all I had in this entire world. I didn't want to lose him."

When she put it like that, Nate could understand. "He was working with the DEA then, wasn't he?"

Megan nodded. "He wanted to put men like the ones who'd sold heroin to me in prison."

She looked down, squeezed her eyes shut, and Nate knew where her thoughts were taking her. What a sick twist of fate it was that John Cross, one of the guards who'd raped her and the other girls, had landed himself a sweet post as an agent with the DEA when he ought to have been serving time in prison. Nate couldn't imagine how Megan must have felt when that son of a bitch showed up on her brother's doorstep.

"I didn't mean to kill anyone." Tears welled up in Megan's eyes. "Marc answered the door, and *he* came inside. I was so afraid! I panicked, just lost it. I ran and hid. Marc came after me. He asked me what was wrong, and it just spilled out of me—what Cross and the others had done to me and the other girls."

"And your brother believed you."

Megan nodded, tears spilling down her cheeks. "He went back to the living room and confronted Cross. I heard them yelling. I heard Cross say that it hadn't been rape, that I had wanted it. He was laughing as if what he'd done to me and the other girls were nothing."

Cross's words, as remembered by Hunter, were part of the court record and had been reported in the paper. Nate remembered them because they'd made him sick.

You know how chick inmates are—bored and horny, dreaming of dick. Every time you walk by their cells, you know they're hoping you'll give it to them.

"I walked out to them. It was like I was sleepwalking. I... I saw Marc's gun on the table, and then it was in my hands. It went off. And then Cross was lying on the floor, and Marc was telling me to run, to go, and I... I ran." Megan covered her face with her hands.

Her quiet weeping tugged at Nate's chest. He knew what it was to kill. He'd taken his share of lives in Afghanistan, had pulled the trigger and watched men die. Ending another person's life was never easy, not even when you'd trained for it, prepared yourself mentally for it. Not even when it was self-defense.

But what Megan had endured ...

Jesus Christ!

Nate would be lying if he'd said he wasn't glad Cross was dead. The bastard had worked hard to earn every one of the three bullets that had ripped through his chest. But Nate wished it hadn't been Megan who'd pulled that trigger—for her sake and her brother's.

Hunter had tried to cover for his sister, taking the blame for Cross's death, hoping his status as an agent and a decorated veteran would net him a plea bargain and short sentence. But the attempt had backfired, and he'd found himself serving life without parole, while Megan, traumatized and tortured by guilt, ended up on the streets once again using heroin to make herself forget. And then she'd ended up in prison, too, already pregnant.

Only after Cross's accomplices had decided to hunt down their victims and silence them one by one had the truth come out. Megan, out on parole, had realized they'd be coming after her and had fled with her baby. Marc, knowing she was running for her life, had taken a woman reporter hostage and broken out of prison to protect Megan. They'd probably be in Mexico right now if it hadn't been for Darcangelo, who'd put the pieces together and tracked them down.

The jury had found Megan not guilty by reason of self-defense, agreeing with her attorney that she had good reason in her state of mind to believe she was in mortal danger. But Hunter's jury had found him guilty on all counts, holding him responsible for covering up the truth about Cross's death—and for taking that reporter hostage.

Megan sniffed, wiped the tears from her face. "Marc was my hero. He did so much for me, but I almost ruined his life."

Nate handed her a tissue, fighting the need to hold her, comfort her. "He was a grown man, a federal agent, a combat veteran. He knew what he was doing, Megan. You can't blame yourself for his choices."

She met Nate's gaze, her green eyes red from crying. "I killed a man, and I let my brother go to prison for it. I could've come forward at any time during the six years he was behind bars, but I didn't. Instead, I lived on the streets doing drugs. I got pregnant by a drug dealer for God's sake—and I barely remember when it happened! How can you look at me with anything but contempt?"

That answered Nate's questions about Donny.

Nate reached out, brushed a strand of auburn hair from her face. "When I look at you, Megan, I see a woman who suffered so much so young. I see a survivor who has fought hard to make a new beginning for herself and her little girl. I see a person who volunteers to help the poor and the homeless because she knows what it's like to live on the streets, a mother who is doing one hell of a job of raising a child alone, a good parent who loves her daughter."

"How can I be a good mother when I was in prison for the first year of Emily's life?" Megan shook her head, tears filling her eyes once more, anguish on her face. "There's no such thing as new beginnings. No matter what I do, it always comes back. Always. There are some things the world just doesn't forgive."

Nate quit fighting his instincts. He drew her into his arms, held her, let her cry, her slender body shaking violently. "It's not so much that the world won't forgive you, Megan, honey. It seems to me that you won't forgive yourself."

CHAPTER 9

"Be careful. It's hot."

"Thanks." Megan took the mug of steaming chamomile tea from Nate, a part of her craving something much stronger.

While he put more wood on the fire, she sipped, struggling to pull the pieces of herself together. She felt drained, weak, ragged. It seemed unreal to her that she'd just bared the darkest side of her soul to a man she'd known only for a week, but she had.

She'd told him everything.

More than that, she'd buried her face in his shirt and sobbed while he'd held her. The only other men she'd let touch her like that were Marc and Julian, but that was different. Marc was her brother, and Julian... Well, he was like a brother.

What she felt for Nate was very different.

She couldn't deny that she was attracted to him. Usually that meant she'd want to run as far away from him as she could. But she wasn't running. And, even stranger, neither was he.

He poured himself another drink and sat on the sofa. "Are you warm?"

She nodded, grateful for the blanket he'd wrapped around her shoulders.

He leaned back into the cushions, his eyes narrowing as he looked at her. "Can I ask you a question?"

"Sure. Why not?" She no longer had any secrets where he was concerned.

"That reporter your brother took hostage when he broke out of prison—he got her pregnant while he was on the run, and she married him, didn't she?"

Nate's question, as blunt as it was, wasn't what Megan had been expecting.

She laughed. "He and Sophie have been married for almost four years now, and they have two kids—Chase and Addison."

Nate shook his head, a bemused expression on his face. "That's … interesting."

Megan smiled. "Believe it or not, Marc can be very sweet. You haven't exactly seen his soft side."

"No, I suppose I haven't." Nate gave a wry grin. "I don't blame him for watching over you the way he does. If I were in his shoes and spotted some strange guy walking up to my little sister's front door after she'd been attacked, I probably would've done the same thing."

"Marc knows I get … uncomfortable around men, and I guess he does his best to make certain I feel safe." Megan looked away, took a sip of tea.

"Do you feel uncomfortable around me?" It was a sincere question, no defensiveness in his voice, no hint that she needed to lie to protect his ego.

Megan found herself studying him, from his short sandy brown hair, to his deep-set blue eyes to the tanned skin on the left side of his face, to the scars on the right. "No—which is kind of strange."

It was both fascinating—and frightening.

"Well, that's good—I think." The smile lines around his eyes crinkled, a hint of humor in his voice.

And she knew she would never get a better time than now to let him know where she stood. "I'm never going to be with a man, Nate. I'm telling you this now because ... because I don't want to mislead you. I don't like being touched. I don't like sex. I've never enjoyed it."

"Never?" His brows bent in a frown.

"Never." She glanced away for a moment, unable to bear the scrutiny of his gaze. "When a man touches me, I feel ... revulsion. I instantly feel sick to my stomach. It's all I can do not to shove him away. What those men did to me—it's a part of me. I can't shake it."

Even years of therapy hadn't changed that. A hug from a male acquaintance, a man's arm around her shoulders, an overly long handshake—they all made her want to pull away and run. She couldn't even go to a male doctor.

"I'm sorry. If I'd known... " Nate's frown deepened. "Did I make you feel that way just now when I held you?"

"N-no." Warmth rushed to Megan's cheeks.

"I'm glad to hear that." He seemed to think about this for a moment as if it were a puzzle he needed to solve. "How about when I caught you when you fell getting off the horse?"

"No." Her cheeks burned hotter.

"What about the times I've held your hand?"

Could he see that she was blushing? God, she hoped not! "No, not then either."

His gaze locked with hers. "And last night—when I kissed you?"

"No." She rushed to explain. "But we were interrupted, and I...
I think maybe there just wasn't time for me to react."

Nate set his drink down on the coffee table. "Do you want to
test that theory?"

Megan's heart took off at a sprint. "Wh-what do you mean?"

"I could kiss you again just like I did last night—soft and
easy—and since we're not going to be interrupted this time, you'll be
able to see whether that sense of revulsion kicks in. If it does, we
stop."

"And if it doesn't?"

He gave her a lopsided grin. "We'll know you just needed to
kiss the right man."

She felt that flutter in her belly again, and time was measured in
heartbeats as he watched her, waiting for her answer. Some part of
her was afraid their little experiment would fail. Some part of her
was afraid it would succeed.

There's no point in trying. You know how this will end, girl.

But did she? Everything had been different with Nate so far.

She drew a steadying breath. "How would we do it?"

"We could do it like we did last night." He spoke matter-of-
factly, as if they were discussing how to change a tire. "I'll sit close
to you and kiss you nice and slow, and we can see how that makes
you feel."

She nodded. "O-okay."

In a single slow motion, he shifted so that he sat beside her, his
face inches from hers, his arm stretched out on the back of the
leather sofa behind her. "You tell me if you start to feel queasy or
repulsed, all right?"

It was hard to think with him sitting so close. "All right."

"Ready?" He reached out, stroked her cheek with the knuckles of his right hand.

"Uh-huh."

Without closing his eyes, he leaned in, brushed his lips over hers again and again and again, the feather-light contact sending shivers through her.

"How are we doing so far?" His eyes looked straight into hers, his voice husky.

"Good." She didn't wait for him this time, but rested her palms against the hard wall of his chest, rose up on one knee, and caressed his lips with hers, increasing the pressure.

More shivers.

His eyes drifted shut, his lashes long and dark. One big hand came to rest on her hip as he steadied her. He caught her lower lip between his, and gave it a soft tug.

Belly flutters.

Her eyes closed, her hands finding their way up his chest and over his shoulders as she drew herself against him, needing to be closer to him, her arms locking behind his neck. She tilted her head, kissed his upper lip, then his lower lip, then the corners of his mouth, her tongue tracing the outline of his lips, her senses stirred by the taste of him, by the masculine scent of his skin, by the hard feel of him. And Megan forgot she'd always been repulsed by this.

All she knew was that she wanted more.

Nate fought back a groan as Megan deepened the kiss, teasing his tongue with tentative strokes of her own, her body soft and pliant, her breasts pressing against his chest. His heart beat hard and fast, scotch mixing with pheromones, running hot through his veins, rushing straight to his groin. He held himself in check, yielding the moment to her, letting her set the pace, wanting her to feel safe, in control.

He would never claim to be an expert on women or sex. While other men on his team had spent every moment of their free time trying to get laid, he'd been a quality-over-quantity kind of man. Still, he knew enough about women to be pretty damned sure she wasn't feeling repulsed or sick to her stomach right now. Her fingers dug into the cloth of his shirt, her heart beating so hard he could feel it against his chest.

He wrapped his arms around her, drew her closer, meeting the strokes of her tongue with his own, until she whimpered. His instinct was to kiss her hard and long, but he didn't want to ruin this for her by moving too fast, so he drew back instead, gave both of them a second to catch their breath. "How do you feel?"

Her pupils were dilated, her cheeks flushed. "Like I want you to kiss me again."

And *that* was the invitation he'd been waiting for.

"*Megan.*" His left hand slid into her silky hair, cradling her head as he claimed her mouth in an all-out kiss.

Her lips parted to give him access, her tongue welcoming his as he teased his way inside her mouth, savoring his first full taste of her.

Jesus!

How long had it been since he'd kissed a woman? Hell, he didn't know. It felt like the first time, a jagged bolt of heat lancing through him from the base of his skull to his balls, awakening his very blood.

He held her tighter, gave in to his need for her, drinking in her taste, her sweet scent, the feminine feel of her body, his hand sliding up the curve of her spine.

She whimpered, trembling in his arms. He gentled the kiss, brushing his wet lips over hers. She moaned in protest, her fingers sliding up into his hair, dragging his head down, pressing her lips to his once again, opening her mouth to him.

He hungrily took what she offered. There had to be a thousand different ways to kiss a woman, a thousand different ways for lips and tongues to meet, caress, tease. He wanted to find every single one of them.

He kissed her slow and deep, then drew away, nipping her lips with the sharp edges of his teeth, teasing the places he'd nipped with his tongue, before taking her mouth hard, exploring the softness of her inner cheeks, the slick velvet of her tongue.

She shifted in his arms, straddling him, holding his face between her palms, her lips leaving a trail of fire across his forehead, down his left cheek, over the bridge of his nose to the disfigured side of his face. And there she stayed, pressing soft kisses against scars that had no nerve endings.

He tried to turn his face away, not wanting to subject her to that ugliness, but she stopped him, their gazes colliding for one brief moment.

"Let me." She took up where she'd left off, kissing him with a tenderness that stunned him.

His heart gave a thud, a single hammer stroke of shock, then picked up, beating so hard he thought it might burst through his chest. Some part of him had hoped that a woman might one day see beyond his scars to the man he was inside. But Megan was doing far more than just ignoring his ugliness. She was *accepting* it with a woman's gentleness, her touch soothing memories of savage pain, grief, loneliness.

Christ!

He fought to breathe as she kissed her way down his cheek to the scarred side of his throat, his battered body able to feel only pressure, not the soft heat of her lips or their wetness. But it was enough. It was more than enough.

He recaptured her mouth, hunger for her surging inside him. His instinct was to get horizontal with her, to draw her beneath him so that he could kiss her and touch her everywhere. But afraid that would kindle memories of violence—and determined to do nothing more tonight than kiss her mouth—he lay back, taking her with him, letting her stretch out on top of him. She came without a hint of reluctance, not even breaking the kiss. He cupped her face between his palms, lifting his head off the arm of the sofa to better meet her lips, his tongue curling with hers, her hair spilling around him in a cascade of scented silk.

He lost all sense of time after that, nothing in his world beyond her breath, her hair, her skin. Drunk on the taste of her, he kissed her until his lips ached, until his body burned for her, until they were both breathless, her whimpers and the soft writhing of her body against his driving him crazy, making him want her in all the sweet ways he couldn't have her. And then he could take it no longer, desire shaking him apart.

He broke the kiss, raising them both into a sitting position. Eyes closed, he simply held her, aware only of the rush of his pulse, the mingled sound of their breathing, the sweet feel of her in his arms. Bit by bit, the world returned around him. The crackling of the fire.

The distant roar of the wind. The bite of his zipper cutting into his still-hard cock.

He kissed her hair, shifted, tried to adjust himself without being obvious, refusing to relinquish his hold on her. He was pretty certain he knew the answer to this question, but he asked it anyway. "So, did I make you queasy?"

She looked up at him through wide eyes, her lips swollen and wet. "I never imagined it could be like that."

He felt a surge of protectiveness—and a primal desire to crush all the men who had ever hurt her. "It's always supposed to be like that."

She looked away, then met his gaze once more, seeming to hesitate. "Can we try that experiment again?"

They tried the experiment again the next morning when they ran into each other in the hallway on their way down to breakfast. They tried it when Jack was busy showing Emily what put the waffling in waffles. They tried it when Jack and Emily were occupied feeding Buckwheat bits of a sliced apple. They tried it when Emily left them alone for a moment in the snow fort Nate had built in the back yard. They tried it sitting in front of the fireplace in the library after Megan put Emily down for her afternoon nap.

Quick kisses. Covert kisses. Slow, deep kisses. Tongue. No tongue.

They tried it all, and every time, the result was the same. Never once, not even for a second, did Megan feel queasy or repulsed. Instead, her pulse raced, her knees went weak, and her blood ran hot.

For the first time in her twenty-eight years, Megan felt desire for a man.

No one had ever made her feel the way Nate did—both completely safe and totally out of control. She wanted to touch him, wanted him to touch her. She wanted to give herself over to the heat of being with him, to see where it would carry them.

And if they ended up having sex?

The idea ran through Megan's thoughts all afternoon, making her belly flutter one minute, filling her stomach with butterflies the next. She wasn't sure whether she'd say yes or no if Nate asked her. A part of her was afraid that her fear and revulsion would return the moment they took off their clothes and got into bed together, and yet she'd give almost anything to be able to enjoy a normal sex life—whatever that was.

Oh, she knew what it felt like to have an orgasm. She was able to do that for herself. But to have sex with a man, to share her body with him and to enjoy it...

In her experience, that kind of sex only happened in romance novels, and she'd quit reading those because the stories only served to highlight what was missing from her own life—love, intimacy, physical pleasure. It had been a long time since she'd even allowed herself to consider the possibility of having a man in her life.

But kissing Nate had opened that door again, made her long for things she'd given up on long ago. Did Nate even want to make love to her? And if he did, was she brave enough to say yes?

This question was still running through her mind when Marc called, interrupting a quick kissing session in the great room.

"No lead on Donny yet," he told her.

Her stomach sank. "So the men you arrested aren't speaking."

"Darcangelo and I managed to get one of the assholes to talk. It seems Donny was selling meth for them and some of the money disappeared. He promised to get it from you, and when they heard about the court settlement, they decided to come after you themselves. They claim they haven't seen Donny since the night he attacked you."

"God, I hope you find him." She didn't want to spend the rest of her life looking over her shoulder.

"Now that these gangbangers are in jail, there's a possibility that Donny will just disappear. If he attacked you for money because they were threatening him, he might decide to leave you alone and get the hell out of Denver while he can."

She hadn't thought of that. "That would be nice."

"How's West treating you? Is everything okay? Do you feel safe?"

"Yes. We're fine. Nate and his dad have been wonderful to us. Emily is having the time of her life. She's gotten to ride a horse a couple of times, and yesterday, we went sledding."

"Good. I'm glad. Call me if you need me." He paused for a moment, and there was noise in the background. "*Shit.* One of these fuckers just tried to kick Darcangelo. I need to go before Julian kills him."

"Be careful!" But Marc had already ended the call.

Nate stood, walked over to her. "They haven't found him yet."

Megan shook her head, the weight of reality settling like lead in her stomach.

"He's gotten lucky so far. That's all. I'm not going to let that bastard hurt you or Emily." Nate drew her into his arms, kissed her. "Come with me. I want you to meet someone."

They got dressed in coats, snow boots, gloves and hats — Nate let her borrow one of his ski hats — and walked out through the garage. The day was bright and cold, a landscape of white stretched out beneath an endless cerulean sky. A frigid wind blew snow through the air, the icy little flakes stinging her cheeks. All around them, mountains stretched toward the heavens, their crystalline summits sparkling in the sunshine.

"It's beautiful!"

"My great-grandfather picked the right spot when he built this place. Watch out. It's slick." Nate took her hand and led her around the barn to a paddock where a single horse stood, munching hay. "This is Chinook."

The big stallion walked over to the fence the moment he spotted Nate, a green blanket over his golden body, his nearly white mane and tail catching in the wind. He gave a snort, his breath rising in a frosty cloud, snow caught on his long, dark eyelashes.

"Hey, boy." Nate held out a carrot, patted the animal's neck.

Chinook was taller than the other horses, his neck and chest thicker and more muscular than Buckwheat's or those of the mares Megan had seen. He seemed to ripple with vigor, all taut muscle and sinew, a tension about him she hadn't felt with the other horses.

"He's huge!" She reached out, patted him on the neck. "He's a palomino, too?"

"A world champion." Nate glanced over at her from beneath the brim of his black cowboy hat, pride on his face. "We charge a twelve-hundred dollar stud fee, and he's usually booked during breeding season."

"How many mares does he, you know… ?" Heat rushed to Megan's cheeks when she realized what she was asking.

Lips that had kissed her until she'd melted—lips she wished she could kiss right now—curved into an amused and sexy grin. "Like I said, he's got a powerful sex drive. He could easily cover a half-dozen mares a day if we let him, but I like to keep him rested, keep the quality of his semen high, so I limit him to no more than three mares a day."

Chinook mated with three different mares a day?

"He must be a happy horse."

Nate chuckled. "Come on, boy. Time for you to get some exercise."

Megan watched as Nate led the stallion into the riding arena and saddled him. Chinook was all energy, snorting and shifting impatiently as Nate took the reins and mounted, clearly eager to be ridden. Megan knew the stallion was strong enough to buck Nate off, to trample him, even to kill him, but there was no doubt as to which of them was in control as Nate urged the stallion into a walk, then a trot, and finally to a slow run, which he called a lope.

Some feminine part of her was thrilled to watch Nate ride, to see his skill in the saddle, his command of the stallion. She was so entranced watching him that it took her by surprise when he reined Chinook to a walk and then a halt in front of her.

"Come on." He reached down for her.

Unafraid, Megan took his hand and, with his help, climbed into the saddle in front of him. He gave a little cluck, and Chinook started off again at a walk. Megan could feel the horse's power beneath her—and the mastery of the man sitting behind her, Nate's hard thighs pressing against hers, controlling the stallion's every movement.

He nudged Chinook to a trot, his left arm going around her waist, drawing her back against the hard wall of his chest. "Relax, honey. Just because he's big and aggressive doesn't mean he's going to hurt you."

And Megan understood that Nate wasn't just talking about the horse.

CHAPTER 10

Nate backed Megan up against the wall, her tongue twining with his as they kissed outside the bathroom where Emily played in the bathtub. The two of them had been making out like teenagers all day. But Nate wasn't a teenager. He was a grown man, a man who'd been celibate for four long years, and his body had some very adult ideas about where all this kissing should lead.

He slipped his left hand beneath the soft cotton of Megan's shirt, his palm sliding over the satiny, warm skin of her belly. He moved slowly, giving her time to take in the sensation, to decide whether she liked it. Her eyes flew open, then drifted shut again, the muscles of her belly jerking at his touch, her body shivering, her reaction giving him the answer he needed.

His fingers found the bottom edge of her bra, traced a line where hard underwire met tender skin. Gratified by her quick intake of breath, he cupped her breast, squeezing gently, a layer of rough lace separating his hand from the hard little bud of her nipple. She arched her back, pressing her breast deeper into his palm, her fingers digging into his back.

God, he was on fire for her. He didn't think he'd ever been this aware of a woman's response, his senses fixed entirely on Megan, her every breath, every sound, every tremor. His blood burned for her, his mind buzzing with lust, his cock aching with what was probably his fiftieth erection of the day.

He tugged her bra down, took her naked breast in his hand, the soft, lush feel of it sending a jolt of heat to his groin, making him moan. He fought the urge to push against her with his hips, willing himself to focus on the velvety texture of her pebbled nipples, the silken weight of her breast, the thrum of her heartbeat beneath his hand.

"*Nate.*" She sighed his name, her eyes squeezed shut, her lips parted.

And Nate wondered if he would survive the night.

No one ever died from a hard-on, jarhead.

He wanted to peel off her clothes and make love to her with his hands, his mouth, his cock. He wanted to make her come again and again, wanted to lose himself inside her. He wanted to make her forget the men who'd hurt her, to replace memories of pain, violation, and fear with memories of shared pleasure, to give back to her every bit of herself that those bastards had stolen.

But things were moving so fast, maybe too fast. They'd known each other for a week, had spent a little more than forty-eight hours in one another's company. And not only was Nate about to suffer a testosterone meltdown, he also cared for her.

She *seemed* to want him as much as he wanted her, responding to every touch, every caress, every kiss as if she, too, wanted to get naked and put his mattress to good use. But making out with him was one thing. Out-and-out sex was something else.

The only solution as far as Nate could see was to keep kissing her, keep touching her for as long as it took until she was truly ready for more.

And if that day never comes?

Well, there were always cold showers.

He lowered his mouth to her exposed throat, licking and nibbling the spot where she was most sensitive, his left hand busy teasing her nipple. Her fingers curled in his hair, her head turning to give him access, her breathing ragged.

"Mommy?"

Megan stiffened, gave a little moan. "Y-yes, sweet pea?"

"Can I come out now?"

Nate withdrew his hand from Megan's shirt and rested his forehead against hers, struggling to rein himself in.

"Okay. I'll be right there." Megan looked up at him, her pupils dark, an expression like pain on her face. She adjusted her bra, then reached up, cupped his scarred cheek. "Don't go anywhere."

He could barely walk with this much wood in his jeans, but he didn't say that. He smoothed his hands down her slender arms. "Hey, we have all the time in the world."

As he watched her disappear into the bathroom, he found himself hoping what he'd just said was true.

Megan lay in the dark beside Emily, her body burning with arousal from the hour she and Nate had spent making out in his bedroom. Oh, but the man was good with his hands! He'd brought her to the brink of orgasm without even getting inside her jeans, the way he'd teased her nipples, driving her to the very edge. Now she was wet and aching—and several rooms down the hall from him.

How are you ever going to get to sleep?

She tried to force her mind off the throb between her thighs, turning onto her side to watch her daughter sleep. Emily looked so peaceful, not a worry in her little world, the sight of her making Megan's heart swell. Her life was so different from Megan's—and for that Megan was grateful. She never wanted Emily to know the loneliness, fear, or violence that she'd grown up with, never wanted Emily to doubt for a moment that her mother loved her, never wanted her to view every man as a predator.

That's how it had been for Megan—never trusting, never being able to let down her guard. A man was a threat simply by virtue of being a man. Until Marc had come back into her life, it hadn't occurred to her that some men might be good people. It was a terrible thing to say, but given what she'd been through…

And now there was Nate. Not only was he a good man—a decorated veteran who donated thousands of dollars of meat to Denver's hungry—he also knew everything there was to know about her and accepted her. She couldn't say why, exactly, but she trusted him. More than that, she wanted him.

She'd never imagined that any man would make her feel the way he made her feel—her blood hot and alive, her skin craving his touch, her body so aroused that she actually wanted him *inside* her. The only thing she'd ever longed for this intensely was heroin, but this wasn't the dark, desperate craving of addiction.

This felt pure and bright and clean.

Megan rolled onto her back and clenched her thighs together, wishing the ache inside her would go away. She'd already taken a hot bath, hoping it would make her drowsy, but it hadn't. She closed her eyes, tried to clear her mind, drew slow, even breaths. But she was no closer to drifting off ten minutes later.

Did Nate want her, too? He certainly seemed to. If the way he kissed and touched her wasn't enough to prove that, the hard bulge he'd had in his jeans was. But rather than asking her to sleep with him tonight, he'd walked her to her room, kissed her—and left her to sleep alone. Maybe he wasn't as interested as he seemed.

What would he do if she went to him—knocked on his door, walked inside and asked him to make love to her? Not that she would or even *could* do any such thing. She hadn't known Nate for very long. She wasn't on the pill. She couldn't even be sure she'd enjoy having sex. If she ended up hating it, she would embarrass both of them and perhaps ruin her relationship with Nate. And the last thing she needed was an unplanned pregnancy or a messy relationship to complicate her life.

Besides, she wasn't that brave.

There would be no turning back from this. In her life, there would always be before Nate and after Nate. He had awakened something inside her. He'd shown her that it was possible for her to enjoy a man's touch, to trust a man. He'd given her something she hadn't even realized she was missing, stripping off the armor she'd built around herself, exposing the longing she'd tried to suppress for so long.

Would it be so wrong of her to go to him, to tell him how she felt? After all she'd been through, didn't she have a right to claim some happiness?

She found herself getting out of bed, slipping into her bathrobe, opening the bedroom door, walking barefoot down the hall. Heart racing, she stood outside his closed door for a moment, reminding herself of all the negative things that might happen if she did this.

This was followed by the realization of what would happen if she *didn't*.

Nothing.

Nothing would happen.

Her life would remain the same as it was now—loveless, sexless, ruled by memories, by fear, by loneliness. She didn't want that, not when Nate was here. Not when he made her feel the way she felt.

You can do it. Be brave.

She raised her hand and knocked.

Nate was about to come, his mind wrapped around thoughts of Megan, his hand wrapped around his cock. His heart was beating hard enough that for a moment he thought he'd imagined it, but then it came again.

A knock on his bedroom door.

Fuck!

He threw back the covers, flicked on his bedside lamp. He grabbed a T-shirt and his boxer briefs off the floor and drew them on. Tucking his throbbing dick inside his underwear, he walked to the bedroom door, wondering whether there was an emergency with the herd or whether Chinook had gotten out of his stall again. Hoping his T-shirt would be enough to hide his damned boner, he opened the door. "Megan?"

She stood there wearing a velvety dark blue bathrobe, her auburn hair tangled around her shoulders. "Can I come in?"

"Sure." He stepped aside, trying to keep his dick out of sight—a losing battle when it was pointing directly at her. "You okay?"

She didn't answer, but reached down, untied her bathrobe, and let it slide to the floor, leaving her standing there in blue and white striped long underwear that clung to her body like a second skin. He was so busy letting his eyes feast on her—the curve of her braless breasts, the rounded shape of her hips, the cleft at the juncture of her thighs—that it took him a minute to realize what this meant.

His heart gave a hard knock. "Megan, I don't think—"

She pressed her fingers to his lips. "Shh."

She stood on her tiptoes, rested her hands against his chest, and pressed her lips to his, her kiss taking him by surprise, making his mind go blank.

He drew her into his embrace, kissed her deep and hard, his conscience taking longer than usual to kick in. When it finally did, he tore his mouth from hers. "Megan, honey, wh-what are we doing?"

Her gaze met his, naked hunger in her eyes. "Making love."

It was a good answer.

Riding a pure surge of testosterone, he crushed her against him, reclaimed the sweetness of her mouth, moving them both toward his bed in an awkward slow dance. Only when he'd drawn her onto the bed beside him did his conscience kick in again. "Megan, honey, mmm... We need to talk."

She didn't seem to want to talk, but kept kissing him. Only when he drew them both into a sitting position and pulled away from her did she open her eyes. She looked down at her hands, her hair spilling over her shoulder to hide her face. "You don't want this."

What she said was so patently untrue it almost made him laugh, but somehow he didn't think laughter would go over too well right now.

He reached over, tucked her hair behind her ear, stroked her cheek with a scarred knuckle. He needed her to understand. "Oh, I *do* want this. More than you know. I just want to make certain this is what *you* really want. Sleeping together—that's a big step. I don't want to dredge up bad memories for you or give you another reason to be afraid of men and sex."

There was more to it than that. He searched for the right words. "You're too important to me to risk rushing this."

Some part of him—the part that was pitching a tent—couldn't believe what he'd just said, his more primal instincts telling him to shut the fuck up and kiss her. But he really didn't want to screw this up.

"Rush it?" She lifted her gaze to his. "I feel like I've waited my entire life for this moment. No one has ever made me feel the way you do."

Her words touched something inside him. So much had been stolen from her—not just her virginity, but her ability to view sex as something positive, a way of sharing trust, pleasure, and affection with a man. She'd suffered through having a baby, but she'd never enjoyed sex. That wasn't just fucked up, it was brutally unfair.

But was *he* the man to do something about it? What if he made it worse?

He caught her chin, looked straight into her eyes. "If we do this, you have to promise me you'll tell me if you start to feel uncomfortable or sick to your stomach, okay? Don't force it."

She nodded. "I promise."

Nate found himself wishing they had planned this so that he could give her what she hadn't gotten—the romance and tenderness a woman deserved her first time. He couldn't give her roses. He couldn't offer her romantic conversation over a candlelit dinner. He didn't have satin sheets on the bed. But he supposed all that shit was superficial anyway.

He would give her the only thing he had—himself.

The question was how to go about it.

He decided to start where they'd left off. "Come here."

She slid into his arms, the two of them stretching out on the bed side by side, soft kisses giving way to passionate ones until both of them were on fire, her body moving against his. He slipped his hand beneath her pajama top, claiming the lushness of her breasts without the annoying obstacle of a bra. Her nipples were pebbled and hard—and exquisitely sensitive. He pinched them, rolled them, tugged them, made slow circles over them with his fingertips, her whimpers and whispered pleas urging him on.

But they'd spent the entire day covering this territory. Enough of this teenage shit. Nate wanted to see and taste what he was touching.

He quit kissing her long enough to peel off her pajama top, his gaze taking in the sight of her. His breath left his lungs in a long, slow exhale. "God, you're beautiful."

Her breasts were firm and full without being overly large, more than enough to fill a man's hand. Her nipples were a delicate shade of salmon pink, their petal-soft flesh drawn tight. He forced her onto her back and lowered his head to suckle her.

Fingers caught in his hair, stopping him. "Can we go... slower?"

He looked into her eyes, and through a pheromone haze, he saw fear. "Slower?"

She sat up. "Lie back. Let me touch you."

It seemed to Nate that his heart stopped.

Some part of him realized *why* she wanted this. It would put her in control, make her feel less vulnerable. But the idea of lying there, his scars exposed…

He had an impulse to end this, to tell her it was just too soon for both of them. It had been one thing to take off his shirt when she was someone he barely knew, a stranger helping him with an injury. It was quite another to bare himself to her when he was lying skin to skin with her here in his bed, when he was supposed to be making love to her, when she mattered so desperately much to him.

Did you plan to have sex with your shirt on, idiot?

He hadn't *planned* this at all.

She seemed to sense his reluctance—and the cause of it. She knelt beside him, her hair spilling over her shoulders, her nipples peeking through the auburn strands. "If you think your scars bother me, you're wrong. In my eyes, you're a hero. Your scars are just proof of that."

He didn't feel heroic at the moment.

Coward.

Nate slowly drew his T-shirt over his head, tossed it onto the floor, then laid back, fighting to relax, his heartbeat a thrum in his chest.

She rested her palm over his heart, then began to explore him, sliding her hand over the scarred right side of his chest and then the left, her touch spreading sparks over his skin, the shock of being touched so intimately making Nate's body shake.

And as his fear slowly eased away, Nate realized he'd been waiting an eternity for this moment, too.

CHAPTER 11

Though Nate tried hard to hide it, Megan knew it wasn't easy for him to share himself in this way. He didn't seem to understand that she found him attractive—even downright sexy. His scars were a part of the attraction because they were a part of *him*.

She ran her hand slowly over his right cheek, trailed her fingers down the scarred side of his neck to his chest. The muscles on the left side were firm, his skin soft and bronzed, coarse curls tickling her palm. His dark nipple was flat and smooth like satin, its center a hard little pebble. The hairless right side of his chest had no nipple, his skin pinched, puckered and creased, some of it almost white, some of it darkly pigmented, some of it with an underlying diamond pattern as if it had once been held in place by mesh. It was harder and stiffer than normal skin, too. But it was *his* skin.

She could see now that the burns went all the way around his right side to his back, dipping below the waistline of his briefs, stretching down his right leg to just above his knee. He'd been burned, front and back, from his cheek to his right thigh.

And beneath his boxer briefs? Was he scarred there, too?

His left thigh also bore a large scar, but it was different, not puckers and creases, but a large, pale rectangle that wrapped around his heavy quadriceps. Was that where they'd taken skin for his skin grafts?

So much pain.

And so much courage.

Other than that first night when he told her how he'd been burned, he hadn't spoken of his service with the Marines, keeping all the horrors he'd seen, all the things he'd done, all he'd suffered quietly to himself. He didn't complain. He didn't show self-pity. He simply endured.

She traced a finger down the uneven line roughly in the center of his torso, where scars met normal skin. She couldn't imagine how much he had suffered, couldn't imagine how any woman could have turned her back on him and left him to face the agony of recovery alone. She felt a sharp surge of protectiveness, wishing she could take all of this away from him.

"There are no nerve endings. I can't feel anything beyond pressure. You don't have to touch—"

"Shhh." She lowered her head, pressed her lips firmly to the place where his right nipple ought to have been, wanting to touch him everywhere, to know all of him, wanting to show him that every inch of him, scarred or not, was precious to her.

He sucked in a breath, tensed, his fingers sliding into her hair. "Megan, I..."

His voice faded as she kissed her way down the taut, scarred skin of his belly, her hands sliding down his sides to his hips, his muscles jerking every time her mouth touched him. But if he couldn't feel her, then why... ?

She glanced up, saw him watching her, a look like pain on his face. And she understood. It wasn't so much that he could *feel* her kisses, but rather just the fact that she was kissing *this* part of him that made him react.

Tears stung her eyes, but she blinked them away, swallowing the lump in her throat as she lowered her lips to him again, the sympathy she felt for him warming to desire as she indulged herself, kissing, licking and nibbling her way back up his belly, across his chest, to his neck. Then she did what he'd done to her so many times today, teasing the sensitive skin beneath his left ear, delighting in the way he shivered.

"Oh, Megan." His hands sought out her breasts, his thumbs flicking their tips, making it terribly hard for her to concentrate. Then one big hand slid down her back and beneath her pajama bottoms to grasp and squeeze her bottom. "When are you going to take these damned things off?"

"Later." She was too busy for that right now—and too nervous.

It was so much easier, so much less frightening, to concentrate on him.

She nipped his earlobe, sucked it into her mouth, bit down, the natural scent of his skin filling her head. It was a warm scent, unmistakably masculine, arousing her even more, an intoxicated feeling swelling inside her. She was drunk on him, his taste, the male feel of him. She wanted to kiss him and touch him—everywhere. She wanted to chase away his pain with pleasure. And—*oh, yes!*—she wanted him to keep doing whatever he was doing with his hands, his touch sending shivers of bliss straight from her aching nipples to her womb.

Had she ever felt anything like this?

No, never.

She stretched out on top him, seeking his mouth, her moan mingling with his groan of satisfaction as their lips were reunited in a deep, hard kiss, his head rising off the pillow to meet her, his right arm encircling her to draw her closer, his left hand still busy with her breast. They devoured each other, tongues tasting with slick strokes, teeth nipping, lips teasing. And still it wasn't enough.

But Megan wasn't sure she was ready for what came next.

Nate was on the brink of insanity. He wanted Megan, and he wanted her now. But he had relinquished control to her, and he was afraid that if he took it back, he would lose her. He'd almost brought it to an end a few minutes ago when he'd forced her onto her back, no doubt reminding her of what the guards had done to her again and again. He understood that now. He wouldn't risk making a mistake like that again.

Tonight was about *her*. It was about proving to her that men weren't all monsters, showing her the tenderness she'd been denied, giving her all the pleasure she deserved. It was about helping her reclaim her own body, her own sexuality.

Then from somewhere in his lust-addled brain, there came a thought. He slid his fingers into her hair, lifted her lips from his, looked into her eyes. "Megan, honey, have you ever had an orgasm?"

She stared down at him, her cheeks flushed, her pupils wide, then looked away. "Yes—by myself."

Well, that was good news—and a good place to start.

He stroked his thumbs over her cheeks. "If you show me how you make yourself come, I'll learn how to please you a lot faster."

Her flushed cheeks turned scarlet, and she gaped at him as if he'd lost his mind. "Do people do that?"

"What—masturbate in front of their partners?" Shit, even saying it made his dick harder—and it was already petrified. "Hell, yeah. A lot of people find it sexy. Everyone is different. You can't flick someone's switch unless they show you where it is."

"What if you think I'm weird?"

He couldn't help but chuckle, thinking of O'Malley's girlfriend who, according to O'Malley, had gotten off as a teen by humping her teddy bear. "Trust me, I won't."

She seemed to consider this for a moment, then she eased herself off of him, pushed the covers aside, and laid down beside him on her stomach, her head and left arm on a pillow, her expression saying, quite clearly, "I can't believe I'm doing this."

He propped himself up on an elbow, trailed his fingers down the skin of her bare back, watching as she tucked her other arm beneath her and slipped her hand inside her pajama bottoms. She closed her eyes, and her arm began making subtle up and down motions, her hips thrusting almost indiscernibly. And the realization hit him.

She'd learned to hide it. She'd had no choice. Between overly zealous parents and cellmates, she'd probably never had the privacy most people enjoyed when getting themselves off. With the blankets drawn up to her shoulders, she would seem to be sleeping, not jilling off.

But she didn't need to hide any longer.

He scooted closer to her, kissed her cheek, tickled the skin of her lower back just above the waistline of her pajama bottoms. "Can I help?"

She opened her eyes. "How—"

"Like this." He answered her question before she could finish asking it, sliding one hand inside her pajama bottoms and cupping her bare ass.

Trailing kisses over the sensitive skin of her back, he stroked the silky mounds of her butt, loving the firm, round feel of her. His motions nudged down her pajamas, revealing her glorious ass to his gaze inch by delicious inch, goose bumps rising on her skin as his fingers slowly made their way toward her warm, wet cleft, massaging and squeezing her as he went. He groaned when he found her. He nudged a finger between her labia and stroked the slick, hot entrance to her vagina from behind.

She moaned at his touch, her thighs parting a bit more, her eyes squeezed shut, her left hand clenching the pillow case.

He forced her pajamas down to her thighs, exposing her ass to his view, kissing and nipping those soft mounds while his fingers did a little recon, trying to figure out exactly what she was doing to herself. It wasn't as easy as it sounded, not because he couldn't find his way around by feel—he hadn't been celibate for so long that a woman's body was terra incognita, after all—but rather because he kept getting distracted by what he was feeling, seeing, smelling.

The dark curls on her labia. Her soft musky scent. The heat emanating from her vagina. The delicate folds of her inner lips. The swollen bud of her clit.

One of her fingers was stroking her clit—that much he could tell—but it seemed to him that she was rocking her hips against the heel of her hand, too, putting pressure on her pubic mound. Well, he could handle that—if she'd allow it.

"Let me." He nudged her fingers aside with his own, began stroking her clit as she had done, quick flicks, slower strokes.

She let out a ragged breath, her bottom lifting up, giving him more room to work.

He kissed his way over her skin until he had a clear view, the sight of her vulva knocking the breath from his lungs. Keeping up the rhythm with his fingers, he watched as her muscles tightened, her hips giving little involuntary jerks as her arousal grew, her clit hard and swollen. He was so close now that he could almost *taste* her.

He kissed her inner thigh. "Let me slide my fingers inside you."

She whimpered. "Oh, yes!"

Leaving her to deal with her clit, he parted her labia, ran slow circles around the hot, wet entrance to her vagina—then slid first one and then two fingers inside her.

She moaned, arched her lower back, raising her ass even higher, her head lifting off the pillow, her eyes still closed, her finger rubbing fast circles over her clit. "*Nate!*"

He shifted until he lay on his stomach between her spread legs, his own legs dangling off the foot of the bed, his face inches from heaven. Then, unable to resist, he did something he was certain no man had ever done for her, something guaranteed not to resurrect bad memories. He nudged his face between her thighs—and tasted her.

She cried out, her spine bowing again.

Oh, she tasted musky and sweet, like sex on a stick, her scent teasing his nostrils. He flicked her clit with his tongue, sucked her smaller inner lips into his mouth, circled her vagina with the tip of his tongue, taking her juices down his throat. But he couldn't get enough—not in this position and not with her pajama bottoms catching his chin.

He yanked down her pajamas and tossed them. "Honey, roll over. Don't hide yourself from me. Let me get closer."

One slender thigh passed over his head as she rolled onto her back, her full beauty laid out before him.

With a groan, he lowered his mouth to her—and feasted.

Megan was lost, shocked to the core by the hot feel of his mouth on her, the sensations coursing through her body almost too good to be real. She curled her fingers in Nate's hair, holding on for dear life as he sucked on her clitoris, tugged on it with his lips, flicked it with his tongue, his fingers working magic deep inside her.

She'd never dreamed anything could feel this good.

She bit her lip, fought to stay in control, but that was impossible, each tug of his lips drawing her closer to the edge, heightening her desperation, until her every exhale became a whimper, pleasure coiling tighter and tighter in her belly.

Unbearable. Incandescent. Sweet.

And then she shattered.

"Oh, *my God*!" She came with a cry, arching off the bed, her body shaken apart by a wave of liquid bliss that seemed to roll on forever. Her vagina clenched around his fingers, the feeling of being stretched and filled adding to the intensity.

And then she was floating.

She lay there, breathless and weak and more than a little astonished. She'd just had the best orgasm of her life—with a man.

With Nate.

She opened her eyes and found him looking up at her from between her thighs, his left hand casually playing with the curls on her pubic mound, his lips pressing kisses to her inner thighs. She felt a hitch in her chest, a surge of tenderness for him, this man who had done so much for her. She didn't understand him—why he'd been so kind to her, why he cared so much—but she was grateful for every moment she'd spent with him.

She reached for him, wanting to give him the pleasure he'd given her, willing to endure the suffocating sensation of having him on top of her, of feeling his weight press down on her, of having his penis stabbing inside her.

But rather than stretching himself out above her, he caught her up in his arms and rolled onto his back, carrying her with him, settling her on top of him, drawing her mouth down to meet his. As if he knew, as if he understood...

Her own musky, wild taste filled her mouth, his kiss demanding everything, taking everything. And she gave—willingly. His body shook with unspent sexual tension, the hard ridge of his erection pressing against her belly, still trapped inside the cloth of his boxer briefs.

Eager to bring him the same pleasure he'd brought her, she kissed her way down the midline of his body to the dark trail of curls that disappeared beneath his briefs. She closed her fingers over the waistband and lifted it over his erection, tugging his briefs down his muscular thighs and dropping them on the floor.

Awed by the sight of him, she stared down at his naked body— and distinctly felt her womb clench. For so long, she'd believed she never wanted to see a penis again, but Nate's body didn't feel like enemy territory. It was *his* body—primal, male, beautiful. And it seemed to her that she was seeing a naked man for the first time.

His penis was thick and long, its purplish tip engorged, its satiny skin gleaming. His testicles lay heavy against his thighs, the sac sprinkled with dark curls. The IED hadn't wounded him here, but it had come terribly close, searing the skin off his hip and upper thigh.

She took him in hand, stroked the length of him from tip to root, gratified by his gasp, by the way his hips jerked at her touch. He was so hard in her hand, the skin velvety soft, a bead of moisture appearing from the slit as she moved her hand up the length of him once more.

He reached down, stilled her hand, his gaze meeting hers. "If you don't stop now, honey, I'm going to embarrass myself. I want to be inside you, Megan. Can you trust me that much?"

She set aside her fear—for him. "Yes."

He reached toward his bedside table, opened a little drawer, and pulled out a...

Condom.

He tore it open, the odor of latex hitting her in the face, reminding her of another place, another time—other men.

"No." The word was out before she realized she'd spoken. "Please, I can't ... "

His frowned, nodded, and tossed the small package into the trash bin by his bed. Then he reached for her, settled her astride him. But he didn't try to enter her. Instead, he grasped her hips and guided her so that she rubbed against the hard length of his erection. "Use my cock this time instead of your fingers."

She balanced her weight on her palms, her fingers splayed on his chest, flexing her hips, dragging herself from the root of his cock to the tip and down again, heat reigniting inside her.

"Oh, Megan, honey." His hands found her breasts again, his fingers tormenting her nipples as she found a rhythm.

She opened her eyes, looked down, and watched herself slide over him, the sight intensely erotic and arousing, her labia enfolding him, his penis glistening with her wetness. And she found herself nearing an unbelievable second climax.

But then she moved her hips an inch too far forward. No longer held down, his cock sprang up, its head poised against her entrance.

She froze.

He grasped her hips. "It's up to you."

For a moment, Megan felt like she stood on the brink of some new threshold. She looked into his eyes—and chose Nate.

Slowly, she lowered herself onto him, her moan mingling with his as his cock filled her inch by hard inch. There was no stabbing pain, only satisfying fullness, a slick, sweet stretch. And as she took all of him inside her a thought struck her, making her breath catch, bringing tears to her eyes.

This is how it's supposed to be.

She looked down into a gaze that burned with need. "Oh, Nate!"

He reached up, brushed a tear from her cheek. "Are you okay, honey?"

She nodded, smiled through her tears—and began to move.

He let out a shuddering breath, his muscles tensing as she ground herself against him. He reached down, grasped her hips, helping to guide her motions, his voice a ragged whisper as he urged her on. "God, yes, honey, ride me!"

Oh, and it was perfect!

She'd never dreamed she would experience this, had never believed it was possible for her to be with a man like this, had never known it could *feel* like this—the slippery friction of him inside her, the erotic ache of being filled, the thrum of naked joy in her chest.

Each thrust felt better than the one before, left her desperate for the next, as he began to match her rhythm, driving into her from beneath, the powerful motions of his hips pushing her closer to the brink.

"*Geezus!*" His jaw was clenched, his brow furrowed as if he were in pain.

And she knew he was in pain, the same kind of pleasure-pain she felt—precious torment, sweet distress, torturous bliss.

She wanted it to end. She wanted it to last forever.

She moved faster, his thrusts syncing with her movements, his cock striking some sensitive place deep inside her. And then it hit her.

"Nate!" She cried out his name, tears spilling down her cheeks as orgasm claimed her once more, golden waves of pleasure washing through her, a baptism of sunlight, making the world new again.

But Nate was right behind her. He groaned, his eyes drifting shut, his body shuddering as he came inside her with deep, hard thrusts.

She collapsed onto him, kissed his chest, the left side slick with sweat. He wrapped his arms around her, drew her close, one hand stroking her hair, his heart thrumming in his chest, both of them breathless.

And as sex cooled into sleep, he kissed her tears away.

CHAPTER 12

Nate checked the girth one last time, made sure the traces were secure, then slipped his hands into his gloves and took the reins from Chuck, who'd helped him hitch Buckwheat to the sleigh. "Thanks, Chuck. I appreciate it."

"Sure thing. Have a good time." Chuck turned back toward the bunkhouse, his gaze lingering on Megan for one moment too long.

Nate and Megan had gone into town with Chuck early this morning to pick up supplies. While Nate had focused on the grocery list his dad had given him, Megan had picked up a packet of emergency contraception, together with a package of spermicidal sponges, their only option for protection between now and when she got a chance to go to the clinic next week. It had bothered Nate to find the foreman watching Megan's every move—something he wondered if he should mention next time he was alone with Chuck.

Nate climbed into the sleigh beside Megan, reins in hand. He looked back over his shoulder to where Emily sat beside his dad, bundled in a bright pink snowsuit and covered with a thick sheepskin. "Are you ready back there?"

"Are you waiting for Christmas to get this show on the road?" his dad barked. "I've got a little girl back here who's hungry for some s'mores. Isn't that right, Miss Emily?"

"Go, Buckwheat!" Emily's tiny voice rang like crystal in the cold mountain air.

Nate shared a smile with Megan, gave Buckwheat a little cluck—and they were off.

The gelding tugged at the traces, his hooves churning up snow as he pulled the little sleigh forward. A tap with the reins, and Buckwheat moved into a trot, the bells on his breast harness jingling merrily.

It was a perfect day. The sun shone down on a landscape of sparkling white, the pine trees garlanded with snow, the high peaks thrusting their summits against the endless Colorado sky. But it wasn't the weather that had set Nate's heart to soaring. Credit for that went to the woman sitting beside him.

Nate looked over at Megan and felt a hitch in his chest. She was laughing, a bright smile on her face, her cheeks pink from the cold, her eyes hidden behind a pair of sunglasses, his mother's old ski hat on her head.

She looked over at him, speaking loudly to be heard above the bells and rustling of the sleigh's runners through the snow. "I've never been in a sleigh before!"

"I promised you a sleigh ride, didn't I? When I make a promise, I keep it."

She ducked her head in an adorably shy way, still smiling. "Yes, you do."

He'd awoken early this morning to find her asleep in his arms, her head pillowed on the right side of his chest. He'd lain there, watching her until the urge to kiss her had become too strong to resist. Then he'd kissed her awake, the two of them making love in the shower, Nate backing her up against the marble tiles, wrapping her legs around his waist, and driving into her until she'd cried out his name. When they had finished showering—and kissing on the bed—she'd gone to her room to get dressed. They'd gone down to breakfast separately, her cheeks flushing bright pink when his dad arched his eyebrows at the two of them and asked whether they'd gotten a good night's sleep.

Subtlety had never been old man's greatest strength, but Nate was in too good a mood to deck him.

Megan was a miracle.

Nate didn't know how else to describe it. He'd met her, and his world had changed. Last night had been the single most amazing night of his life. He'd reveled in watching her come alive under his touch, had been humbled by the depth of her trust, had found himself with a huge lump in his throat when she'd come, tears spilling down her cheeks. And when at last he'd climaxed inside her, he had felt reborn.

Though he knew he ought to slow down, he couldn't keep himself from imagining a future with her, the two of them raising Emily together here at the Cimarron, teaching her to ride, maybe giving Emily a sister or brother one day.

"Look!" Megan pointed toward a dark shadow among the trees.

"A bull elk."

"Do you see that, Miss Emily?" Nate's dad asked.

"A deer," Emily offered.

"Nope, he's an elk. Can you say elk?"

"Ewk."

"Good enough."

The animal—a big guy with a six-point rack—took a good look at them and darted deeper into the forest, probably frightened by the bells.

Nate turned to Megan. "It's been a long time since we've hitched up this sleigh—since before my mother died."

"This is magical." She slipped her gloved hand out from beneath the blanket he'd wrapped around her and tucked it in his lap. "I feel like I'm in a living Christmas card."

"And it's not even Thanksgiving yet." He found himself smiling again.

He turned Buckwheat toward the snow-packed lane that led to their destination—the stone picnic shelter he and his dad had built when Nate was sixteen. It had a slanted roof, a flagstone floor, an enormous fireplace, four walls and two windows, but the door and windows were wide open, letting the outdoors in. Nate's dad had packed a lunch of fried chicken and potato salad, but what they were all looking forward to was the hot chocolate and the s'mores.

"It's so beautiful up here, so peaceful."

Nate looked over, smiled at the look of wonder on Megan's face. "You're welcome to come up here any time, you know. I hope you will."

Her smile grew tight, and she looked away.

Megan couldn't remember the last time she'd had more fun. They ate their picnic lunch before a roaring fire that Nate built, then made s'mores, a treat Megan hadn't enjoyed since she'd been a little girl at church camp. After the marshmallows and chocolate were gone, they built a snowman. Then Jack let Emily show him how to make snow angels. Before they were finished,

Emily had them all making snow angels, and the meadow around the picnic shelter was covered with them.

Yet, through it all, some part of Megan was waiting for the other shoe to drop.

She'd never been this happy. All of her dreams had seemed to come true overnight, every closely guarded longing in her heart fulfilled. A deep sense of safety. A man who accepted her despite her past, who seemed truly to care about her and Emily—and who came with a built-in grandfather for her daughter. Soul-shattering sex.

Though she told herself that she had every right to be happy, she couldn't shake the feeling that the dream was about to end. Nate would realize he could do better than an ex-con for a lover. Or Jack would put his foot down and tell his son that it was one thing to give her a safe place to stay for the weekend but quite another to get involved with her. Or the cops would show up, tell her they'd uncovered an old arrest warrant for some case she'd caught eons ago, and arrest her in front of everyone.

She tried to silence the negative thoughts as they climbed aboard the sleigh and headed back to the house, the beauty of the mountains and the cheery sound of the sleigh bells lulling her fears to sleep.

They reached the house late in the afternoon. While Nate took care of the horse and sleigh, Megan put Emily down for a nap and began to pack their things, getting ready for the long drive back to Denver, her anxiety returning. She'd just closed her suitcase when he came up behind her.

"I wish you could stay." He spoke softly so as not to wake Emily, his arms going around her waist, drawing her back against him.

Megan pulled away. "The roads are open, and I'd like to get home before dark."

"My dad can take the two of you in his SUV, and I can follow behind in your car, if you want. I know these roads aren't fun in the snow."

She turned to face him, touched by his selflessness. "That's awfully sweet of you, but I couldn't ask you to do that. That's not a fun way to spend your Sunday night."

"Hey, it's my Sunday night. At least that way I'd know you made it back safely." Nate caught her hand in his, raised it to his lips, kissed it. "And you don't have to ask. I offered."

It would make Megan feel a lot safer to be in a four-wheel drive instead of her little Honda. "Okay. And thanks."

"You know," he said moving closer, drawing her into his arms, "you could stay the night, and we could take you in first thing tomorrow morning."

She felt a little trill of excitement at the idea of another night in his bed but shook her head. "I have to make sure I get to work on time. I can't afford to get fired. It's really hard for people with prison records to find jobs."

She tried to pull away again, but he stopped her.

"Hey, what's wrong?"

She looked away, unable to meet his gaze. "Nothing... I'm just..."

He threaded his fingers through hers and led her out into the hallway, shutting the door behind them. "Something's been bothering you all day. Do you regret last night?"

Megan gaped at him. "No! God, no!"

He let out a slow breath. "Well, I'm glad to hear that at least, because last night was one of the best nights of my life."

"Really?" She felt the same way, but hearing him say it…

She'd never been a part of anybody's best anything.

He caught her chin, tilted her head back so that he was looking straight into her eyes, his thumb stroking lazily over her cheek. "Yeah. Really."

He brushed his lips over hers, claiming her mouth in a slow, sweet kiss that cleared her mind of everything but him.

"Ahem." Behind them, Jack cleared his throat. "Sorry to intrude, but Chuck says something's wrong with Baby Doe. He thinks it's a torsion."

Nate's head jerked up. "What?"

Megan could see from the alarm on his face that this was serious.

"I called Doc Jackson already but… "

"*Shit.*" Nate kissed Megan's hair. "This is a real emergency, honey."

She nodded. "Go."

She watched him disappear down the hall with his father, her lips still tingling.

A n hour later, her suitcases already loaded into her car, Megan sat in the great room watching Emily play with her pony on the coffee table, the scent of homemade spaghetti sauce wafting in from the kitchen. Jack had insisted they stay for supper, and since he and Nate were driving, Megan had agreed. Besides, Jack was an incredible cook.

Still, she was beginning to feel restless, needing to get home, needing to be alone so that she could sort through the confusion inside her.

There'd been no word from Nate about Baby Doe or her foal. Jack had explained that sometimes, late in pregnancy, a mare's uterus could twist, cutting off the blood supply to the foal. Unless they were able to correct the problem, they could lose both the foal and the mare. Megan remembered Baby Doe's beautiful coloring, her soft muzzle, her quiet whickers as they petted her and fed her carrots. She couldn't stand to think of such a beautiful animal suffering.

On edge, she stood, walked toward the fireplace, and found herself looking at the family portrait on the mantel again. How happy the three of them looked together. Nate's mother had been such a beautiful woman, her eyes alight with happiness. She had an unmistakable air of class and sophistication about her, from the way she wore lipstick, to her elegant clothes, to her lovely mabe pearl earrings.

Megan felt shoddy by comparison, cheap. She couldn't help but wonder what Nate's mother would think about his interest in her. For that matter, what did Jack think?

Megan *knew* he knew they'd slept together. His comment at breakfast had proven that. But she had no idea how he felt about it.

She heard men's voices in the kitchen. Thinking Nate was back and might have some news of the mare, she walked toward the kitchen, then froze.

"She's that fugitive's sister." It was Chuck, the foreman, speaking in a hushed voice. "Remember from a few years ago? She's a drug addict. She served time in prison for killing someone, I think.

You don't want her sleepin' with our Nate. He can do a lot better than that."

Blood rushed to Megan's head, her pulse rocketing. Chuck had been there this morning when she'd bought the morning-after pill. He must have seen...

A lid clanked against a pot.

Jack spoke. "Let's go into my office and talk about this."

Not wanting to be caught eavesdropping, she hurried back to Emily and just managed to sit on the sofa when Jack and Chuck emerged from the kitchen, heading toward Jack's office.

Jack looked over at her, an angry frown on his face.

She felt a tearing sensation in her chest, the pain sharp and cold. A hard lump formed in her throat, dropping straight into her stomach as she watched him disappear down the hallway, his foreman behind him.

She had humiliated him. She'd brought embarrassment to Jack and to Nate in their own home, exposing them to gossip from the ranch hands.

Once again, her past had caught up with her.

And then it was just too much.

She found their coats by the front door, grabbed her purse and Emily's mittens off the table in the foyer, fighting back tears. "Come, sweet pea. It's time to go."

The dream was over.

Nate stroked the anesthetized mare's flank, felt the foal moving inside her. Thankfully, it hadn't been a complete torsion. Doc

Johnson had been able to rotate Baby Doe's uterus back into place vaginally, sparing her surgery. But they were going to have to watch her closely until she foaled.

"I've got a hunch as to what caused this." Doc Johnson pulled the shoulder-high exam glove off his arm. "Either that foal is huge, or she's carrying twins."

Nate stared up at him. "You did an ultrasound. There was only one embryo."

"Hey, once in a while even I make a mistake. Let's have another look."

Nate waited with the mare, checking her IV tubing, while Doc Johnson went to retrieve his ultrasound machine from his truck.

Five minutes later, he found himself staring at a blurry black-and-white image of not one, but *two* foals. Two hearts beating, two heads, two rumps, eight hooves. Definitely twins.

Shit.

Twin foals rarely survived.

Doc Johnson withdrew his gloved arm and the ultrasound wand from the mare's rectal cavity and rolled off the glove. "Everything looks good so far, but that's far from a guarantee that either foal will survive. Our priority, of course, will be the mare. Let me get on the horn with the equine folks at CSU. I would advise boarding her at the hospital until this is over. I know Fort Collins is a long drive, but she needs around-the-clock observation."

Nate nodded, still stroking the horse's flank. Losing the foals would be one thing. Losing Baby Doe would be something else. "Thanks, Doc."

Nate heard footsteps and looked up to see his dad approaching, a worried look on his face. He filled the old man in on what Doc

Johnson had told him. "I'll ask Chuck to get a trailer ready. We've got to get Megan home before—"

"Yeah, well," his dad scratched his head, a sheepish look on his face. "We've got a problem, son."

Nate didn't like the sound of that. He stood. "Oh, yeah?"

"Megan's gone."

S he shouldn't have run. The moment she'd reached the highway, Megan had realized that. She should have stayed, stood her ground, proved to Jack that the past couldn't chase her away. Instead, she'd panicked. She'd grabbed Emily, and she'd run. She'd been so afraid of facing Jack, so afraid of how he and Nate would react, that driving in the dark on snowy mountain roads had seemed the easier course. What a coward she'd been!

She hadn't even bothered to say thank you or good-bye.

Oh, Nate, I'm so sorry.

She turned onto her street, her neck and shoulders stiff, her head aching from an hour and a half of white-knuckle driving, her stomach sick with regret. All she wanted now was to get supper made and Emily to bed so that she could call Nate and apologize to both him and his father. She would have called him already, but she'd left her cell phone in their house somewhere—which meant she would see Nate at least one more time.

Pushing the button on her garage door opener, she pulled into her driveway, grateful to Marc for shoveling while she'd been away. She needed to call him from her landline and tell him she was safely home so that he could send a surveillance team over to watch the house.

She glanced in the rearview mirror to find Emily sound asleep. And no wonder. The sweet little dear had thrown a temper tantrum when Megan had tried to buckle her in her car seat, kicking and screaming because Megan wouldn't take her to say goodbye to Buckwheat. Megan had felt like the worst mother *ever*.

"Emily, sweet pea, we're home."

Emily stirred, opened her eyes, glanced around, looking sad and grumpy. "Are we going to see Buckwheat again?"

Megan didn't know how to answer. She parked the car, closing the garage door behind them. "We sure had a fun time up at the ranch, didn't we? Right now, we're going to have some supper and get settled in for the night. I have to go to work in the morning, and you have preschool."

Megan had no idea what she was going to make for supper. She didn't have the energy to cook. Maybe she ought to just drop off her laundry, grab a few things and head over to Marc and Sophie's and spend the night there. But then Marc would ask questions, and she would end up having to explain things she shouldn't have to explain.

She got out of the car, opened the rear passenger door, and unbuckled the harness on Emily's car seat, scooping her daughter, toy pony and all, into her arms. She set Emily down outside the door that led from the garage to the kitchen, unlocked it, and let Emily inside, flicking on the light. "You go hang your coat on the hook and put your boots by the front door, okay, sweet pea? I'm going to get our suitcases."

She walked to the trunk of the car, opened it with a click on her keychain, and lifted out the two suitcases, trying to think her way through the evening. She needed to call Marc first thing. Then she would make dinner, get Emily into the tub, and after Emily was asleep, she would call Nate. As for supper, she could unthaw some chicken breasts and bake them with a bit of marinade. Or given how late it was, maybe she should just grab another jar of sauce and make spaghetti again.

It would be nothing like Jack's spaghetti.

How funny that she'd been so restless to get home, and now that she was here, she wished with all her heart she could relive these past two hours and stay at the Cimarron.

Feeling weighed down by more than luggage, she walked inside and set the suitcases down, shutting and locking the door behind her. She was about to reach for the phone, when she noticed it...

A strange smell—like a faint whiff of burned plastic.

And there were dirty dishes in the sink.

She hadn't left the house like that. She hadn't....

The adrenaline hit just as Donny stepped into the kitchen, Emily in his arms, one filthy hand clamped over her mouth.

"I've been waiting for you, Megan." He laughed. "Oh, come on! Don't just stand there staring at me. Come give your sugar daddy a big kiss."

CHAPTER 13

Megan's mouth went dry, her heart thudding sickeningly in her chest. Her mind raced, looking for a way out of this, but all she could see was the terror in Emily's eyes—and the tinge of meth-fueled mania in Donny's.

Think! Think! Think!

A knife?

No, he would use it against her—or maybe threaten Emily.

Try to take Emily away from him?

No, Emily might get hurt in the scuffle.

Grab the phone and dial 911?

Megan didn't dare as long as Donny had her daughter.

If only she hadn't forgotten her cell phone, she might have been able to text Marc or dial 911 with the phone in her pocket. There was a phone in her bedroom. If she could get Emily away from him and lock herself in her room…

Donny sneered at her, his face beaded with sweat, his body jittery. "Your asshole brother thought I couldn't find you, but here I am. I waited till you left, and he called off the cops. Then I came in through the crawl space—and just made myself at home."

Something in his eyes, in the tone of his voice, warned her not to show fear.

She swallowed, tried to speak in a cold but calm voice. "It... It's not polite to drop in without calling, Donny. I haven't even made dinner yet. How does chicken sound?" She crossed the kitchen to the fridge, opened the freezer door, and took out a packet of chicken breasts, her pulse a thrum in her ears. "Emily, go wash up for supper."

Out of the corner of her eye, Megan saw the look of confusion on Donny's drug-worn face. He did nothing to stop Emily as she kicked and wriggled her way to the floor.

But rather than going to the bathroom, as Megan had hoped she would, Emily ran straight to her and threw her arms around Megan's legs.

Megan scooped her up, held her tight, then reached with one hand to put the frozen chicken in the microwave, her fingers pushing some sequence of numbers—she didn't know what—on the keypad. "It's okay, sweet pea. It's okay. I'm right here."

She needed to get Emily away from Donny somehow.

"While this thaws, let's go hang up your coat and get your hands washed, okay? Donny, when that beeps, take it out. If you're going to eat my food, the least you can do is help—and clean up your own dishes." As she turned to walk to the bathroom, she glanced down at the full sink—and froze.

Her Pyrex baking dish was ringed by a dark stain, her stainless steel stock pot crusted with something, the drinking glasses...

They weren't drinking glasses. They were ... beakers? Beneath them sat a length of coiled plastic tubing and...

Oh, my God!

He hadn't been cooking food. He'd been cooking up meth.

The funny smell.

She had to get Emily out of here. *Now.*

She walked passed him, praying that he would be too confused to guess what she was doing. If she could only make it to her bedroom, she could lock the door and call—

Bony fingers grabbed her arm.

"You think I'm stupid?" The nauseating stench of his rotting teeth and body odor hit her full in the face. "You're going downstairs—both you and the kid."

Megan tried to jerk her arm away. "I have to get my daughter out of here. You've been cooking meth in my house! That stuff is toxic! Every second we're in here, she's breathing—"

"Shut the fuck up!" A gun appeared in his hand. "Turn off the lights, take the brat, and go downstairs."

Fear slid like ice into her veins.

If pressed, Donny would use the weapon—of that she had no doubt. He had once attacked Marc with a knife.

"I-I'm taking food." Megan couldn't keep the quaver out of her voice. She turned toward the pantry and managed to grab a box of granola bars before Donny shoved her. "She's hungry. She needs to have her supper."

"There's food downstairs." He flicked off the kitchen lights, leaving the house in darkness. "Now go!"

Megan felt her way to the stairs, swamped by a sense of déjà vu, an all too familiar feeling of despair, of helplessness. "What do you want? Why are you doing this?"

"Shut up!"

Megan walked down the stairs on unsteady legs, Emily's face buried in her neck. "It's going to be okay, sweet pea. Just do exactly what Mommy tells you to do, okay?"

She heard Donny close the door behind them, the sound ominous—a trap swinging shut.

The basement was a mess. Plastic bottles of chemicals sat near the stairs, rocks of crystal meth on the coffee table, a bag of potato chips lying discarded on the floor beside a banana peel, empty beer bottles, water bottles, and jackets from dozens of porn DVDs. The television was on, the graphic image of a man's penis inside a woman's vagina frozen on its screen.

Of course there would be porn. Donny had always loved it.

Relieved that Emily hadn't seen, Megan quickly turned the TV off, then carried her daughter to the play corner and sat on the carpet beside her dollhouse, holding Emily in her lap. "Do you see that stuff on the coffee table, Emily?" she whispered. "It's poison. It's very bad. Don't touch it! Don't eat it! Do you hear me?"

Emily nodded, tiny tears on her cheeks.

"Hey, did I say you could turn off the TV?"

Megan glared at him. "I won't let you expose my daughter to that kind of filth, even if you do have a gun."

He sat down on the couch, his gazed fixed on Emily. "She's my daughter, too."

Megan cringed at his words, held Emily tightly against her chest, hoping Emily hadn't understood. "What do you want? Money to pay off the gangbangers who were after you? They're in jail."

He frowned, looked confused.

"You didn't know? Marc caught them."

Donny's eyes narrowed. "You're lying."

"No, I'm—"

"*Shut up!*" His shout made Emily cry and Megan jump. He bolted to his feet, sweat trickling down his temples. "Now, here's what's going to happen. Tomorrow morning, you're going to go to the bank and withdraw every penny you have while I stay here with the kid. When I have the money, I'll go. But if you take off or you try to come back with your brother or the cops, I'll shoot the girl. I gave her to you. I can take her away. Got it?"

Megan thought she might throw up. "Yes."

"Good." Donny sat again, his body visibly twitching. "We'll just have ourselves a little night together—a family reunion."

Nate parked in front of her house, surprised not to find an unmarked police car on the street. If he'd been Marc Hunter, he wouldn't have taken his eyes off Megan until that bastard Donny was either dead or behind bars.

Nate got out of his pickup, Megan's cell phone in his pocket, and walked toward the house. The sidewalk and driveway had been shoveled, but the house was dark, the curtains drawn. There was no sign that anyone was home, apart from the trail of snow her tires had left on the concrete driveway when she'd driven into her garage.

He rang the doorbell.

Nothing.

He waited, rang again.

Nothing.

Damn it!

Nate's dad had come straight out to get him the moment he'd realized Megan was gone. The old man had known exactly *why* Megan had left so abruptly. Nate had called her right away, hoping to explain, but she hadn't answered. Only after he'd called from the kitchen and had heard her phone ringing upstairs had he realized why. The cell phone had given him an excuse to follow her. He'd left his father in charge of the situation with Baby Doe and had come after her, but by then she'd been halfway back to Denver.

Right now, Nate wasn't sure whose ass he wanted to kick more—his own for rushing things, for pushing Megan too far, too fast; his father's for allowing Chuck to wag his tongue with Megan in the other room; or Chuck's for getting involved in something that was none of his damned business. Yeah, Chuck meant well. He'd been with the Cimarron since Nate was a kid. But that didn't mean he could offer his two cents on Nate's love life. At the end of the day, he was an employee, and he needed to remember that.

Nate stared at the closed door.

Maybe she's not answering because she doesn't want to see you.

The thought put a fist-sized hole through his chest.

He found it hard to believe she would let him stand here on her front steps after last night. He could understand her being hurt and upset by what she'd heard Chuck say. He could even understand her packing up and leaving. She probably thought she was doing them a favor, getting out of the house to spare them shame or some damned thing.

But to ignore him? No, he couldn't understand that.

Megan, don't do this to yourself. Don't do this to us.

It shouldn't matter to her what Chuck or anyone else thought. What mattered was what she and Nate felt.

Seconds ticked by.

Then it occurred to him that she might have come here and then left to stay at her brother's house. That would explain the lack of a surveillance unit on the street—and why the house was dark.

He turned to go, hesitating on her front steps. Something about the situation didn't feel right, but he couldn't put a finger on it. He glanced around, his senses trained on the darkness.

Nothing.

He walked back toward his truck, climbed in, and headed down the street, wondering how her brother would feel about his dropping by.

"**Y**ou hear that? Whoever it was, they just drove away." Donny chuckled, bent down until he was looking into Megan's eyes, his grin exposing missing and blackened teeth, the foul reek of his mouth overpowering. "With the lights out upstairs, nobody knows you're here."

What little hope Megan had evaporated, fear churning in her stomach. When she'd heard the doorbell, she'd thought for certain it must be Nate or Marc coming to check on her. She'd felt sure that if they saw the lights were out, they would know something was wrong. It hadn't occurred to her that they would think she wasn't home.

Donny walked back to the couch, sat, and picked up his pipe, dropping a blue-white rock of meth into the bowl and reaching for his lighter.

"No! Please don't smoke any more of that in front of us." She'd watched him binge on meth for the past hour, his actions toward her growing more and more aggressive. "I don't want Emily breathing the fumes."

He turned to look at her, his gaze dropping briefly to Emily, who sat silently in Megan's lap, clutching her toy pony. "It won't hurt her. Besides, I've *got* to have it."

Megan had never done meth, but she remembered feeling that way, her veins hollow and screaming, her head pounding, her body aching for that next fix of heroin. Helpless to stop him, she turned Emily away from the smoke, a faint chemical smell like burning plastic in the air. "Why don't you play over here, sweet pea? Mommy doesn't want you breathing that—"

Donny groaned. "Fuck! Fuck, yes! Aaah, yeah!"

Megan covered Emily's ears, looked over, saw a euphoric expression on Donny's face and felt chills slide down her spine as his gaze shifted—and locked with hers.

He grinned. "Either you need to let me turn this TV back on, or you need to get over here and give my dick what it really wants."

"No! There is a four-year-old child here." *Four years old.* That's the age Megan had been the night her life fell apart. "You're just going to have to go upstairs if you want to do *that* with yourself. There's another TV in the living room."

Wired from the drug, Donny fidgeted, his gaze still on her. "Do you remember how I used to take care of you, Megan? I took you in. I fed you. I got you whatever you needed—clothes, drugs, makeup. Do you remember that? Now you think you're too good for me, don't you? You're not. You might have a house and a car and a brother who's a cop, but you're still the same little smack whore."

Megan felt heat rush to her face, rage chasing her fear way. "You *used* me. You gave me drugs, and you used—"

In the blink of an eye, he was on his feet and moving toward her.

Megan put Emily behind her. "Hide, Emily."

Donny fisted his hands in Megan's hair, jerked her to her feet, pointed the gun in her face. "After all I did for you, you owe me."

Not this. Not rape again!

"But my baby girl—"

"Tell her to close her eyes if you don't want her to watch." Donny dragged Megan to the couch, pressed the gun to her face, and pushed her back onto the sofa, one hand dropping to the zipper of her jeans.

Emily started to cry. "Mommy! Mommy!"

"Mommy's okay, sweet—"

"Tell her to shut the fuck up!" Donny turned, pointed the gun at Emily, who cried harder. His hands were shaking, his finger on the trigger. "Shut up! Shut up! Shut *up!*"

Oh, God Emily!

"No!" Megan grabbed him, tried to turn the gun away from her daughter. "Please, no! Don't—"

BAM! BAM!

Megan's heart seemed to stop, fractured images filtering to her mind through a haze of adrenaline.

Donny jerking out of her grasp, pitching headfirst over the back of the couch.

His gun falling.

Blood spattering her shirt, the couch, the wall.

And then Nate was there.

He touched a reassuring hand to Megan's shoulder, then hurried over to Emily, scooped her into his arms, and carried her back to Megan. "Everything's going to be okay, sweetie. It's over. Here's your mommy."

Megan reached up, took Emily from Nate's arms, held her tightly, her body shaking with relief. "Oh, Emily! Oh, my sweet girl! It's okay, sweet pea. It's okay."

Nate's strong arm went around Megan's shoulder. He drew her to her feet. "Can you walk? Can you carry her?"

Megan nodded. "Yeah."

"Let's get the two of you out of here."

"How'd you know something was wrong?" Darcangelo asked. Nate walked across the hospital parking lot with Hunter and Darcangelo, the two of them having helped him retrieve his pickup truck from Megan's house. He'd already spent at least two hours being debriefed by homicide detectives—who had confiscated the SIG for forensic purposes, leaving him down yet another firearm—and now he wanted to see Megan and Emily with his own eyes, make sure they were okay.

"All the lights were out—not just the lights inside the house, but also the outdoor security lights. I knew Megan wouldn't turn them off." He'd been halfway down the block, looking at her house in his rearview mirror, when it had hit him. "I stopped, went back, found tracks in the snow leading up to the entrance for the crawl space and signs of forced entry. So I called you—and went in."

Hunter clapped him on the back. "I told you to wait, but I'm damned glad you didn't."

So was Nate.

He'd seen a lot of twisted shit in his life, but nothing that had shaken him as much as seeing Donny point that S&W .38 special at Megan's face—and then turn it on Emily. He'd hoped to get them out of there without bloodshed, but in that moment, he'd known he had no choice but to fire, five pounds of pressure and a 9mm hollow-point round ending Donny's wasted, meaningless life.

Hunter stopped outside the ER entrance. "Did you disobey orders like that in the Marines?"

Nate chuckled. "No, but Hunter?"

"Yeah?"

"Just to be clear, *you* don't give me orders." Nate reached for the door handle.

Darcangelo chuckled. "I think you've been handed your ass, Hunter."

"Shut up, Dickangelo."

Nate ignored the bickering newlyweds and walked quickly through the ER, the bright fluorescent lights a sharp contrast to the darkness outside. With the help of Hunter's wife Sophie, a pretty strawberry-blonde, he convinced the nurse he was Megan's partner, and was led to an exam room where Megan was resting and awaiting discharge, Emily asleep in her arms.

"Hey." Megan was wearing hospital scrubs, her clothing either taken as evidence or confiscated due to exposure to hazardous chemicals from the meth. There was an adhesive bandage in the bend of her arm where they'd apparently drawn blood. Her eyes were swollen and red from crying, but she smiled when she saw him, reaching for him with her free hand. "I'm so glad you're here."

That was nice to hear.

He took her hand, kissed it. "How are you feeling?"

"I'm fine... now." She looked down at her daughter, stroked Emily's hair. "And Emily is going to be okay, too. They don't think we were there long enough for the chemicals to have done any lasting damage."

"I'm relieved to hear that."

Megan looked up at him, tears welling up in her eyes. "Thank you. If you hadn't showed up when you did, Donny would have... "

"I know." Nate moved to her side, drew her head against his chest, kissed her hair, the feel of her precious in his arms. "I know."

He held her while she wept, wishing he could erase all memory of the past five hours for her and for Emily. But he couldn't.

Megan sniffed, but she didn't try to pull away. "When your gun fired, I... I thought it was Donny's. I thought... I thought he'd shot Emily."

"I'm so sorry. I didn't have a chance to warn you."

She tilted her head back, looked up at him. "No, please don't apologize. You saved her life. You saved mine. I... I just didn't know you were there."

"I came in the same way he did—through your crawl space. It empties out behind your furnace. Did you know that?"

She shook her head. "It doesn't matter now. I won't be going back there again."

She had a long road ahead of her there, as state law mandated the cleanup of meth labs to such a degree that sometimes the only real option was to demolish the home and rebuild. But whatever she had to do, Nate wouldn't let her face it alone.

"I'm sorry, Nate." She drew away, looked up at him, took his hand. "I'm sorry I left the ranch the way I did. I... I heard Chuck telling your father the things he'd read about me in the newspaper, and your father looked so angry. I couldn't stand to think my being there was leaving you open to gossip, so I... "

"Ran."

Her gaze fell. "So I ran."

"My father *was* angry—at Chuck." Nate sat in the chair beside the bed, bringing his face to her level. "He took Chuck to his office to tell him to mind his own damned business. But I think that was just an excuse, Megan. I think you'd been looking to run anyway. I could feel it—you drawing away from me minute by minute all day. Why, Megan?"

Tears welled up in her eyes again, spilled down her cheeks. "Did you ever have anything you wanted so much that when you got it, it didn't feel real?"

"Yeah." Nate had felt that way when she had kissed his scars.

"I care about you so much, Nate. But my past—it follows me everywhere. After last night, I... I just couldn't wait around for the moment when you realized you don't want ... someone like *me*... in your life."

"Oh, Megan." Nate cupped her cheek in his palm. "You saw beneath my skin and accepted the man I am, scars and all. Why is it *so hard* for you to believe that I can accept your scars, too?"

She stared at him as if in amazement, then laughed through her tears. "You really mean that, don't you?"

"Hell, yeah, I do." He leaned in, kissed her. "I'm not asking for forever right now, but I *am* asking for tomorrow. Promise me you'll *try*. Promise me you won't give up on whatever this is between us— not till we've given it everything we have. I won't let you down."

"Oh, Nate!" She looked straight into his eyes. "I promise."

Megan carried a drowsy Emily out to the parking lot, Nate on one side of her, Sophie and Marc on the other. She wanted nothing more than to crawl into bed with her baby girl and sleep— for a week, if possible. Her boss had given her the next few days off, insisting she take time to recover. Since Thanksgiving was Thursday, that gave Megan a full week to recuperate—and figure out where she was going to be living for the next few months until she could decontaminate and sell her house.

Julian was waiting outside for them. "How are you doing?"

"Uncle Julie?" Emily stirred sleepily.

"Hey, sweetie, I'm here. You look like a little girl who's ready for bedtime." Julian turned to Marc. "Your SUV's warming up over there."

Megan was about to say goodnight to Nate when a pickup hauling a horse trailer pulled into the parking lot beside them, the letters C and R painted on its side.

Nate stared. "What in the hell does the old man think he's doing?"

Jack climbed out and walked toward them, wearing a sheepskin barn jacket, a gray cowboy hat on his head.

Emily perked up in Megan's arms and reached for him. "Jack!"

"Good evening there, Miss Emily." He hugged her, then met Megan's gaze. "I was sorry to hear about what happened. I'm glad you're alright."

"Thank you."

Megan introduced Jack to everyone and everyone to Jack.

"I feel like I'm meeting a celebrity," Jack said when he shook Marc's hand. "I had that wanted poster up on the barn wall for months."

Marc grinned. "Want me to autograph it for you?"

But Jack's attention was on Emily again. He motioned for them to follow him. "I brought someone to see you, Miss Emily."

Megan looked to Nate.

Nate shrugged. "He's supposed to be driving Baby Doe to the equine hospital at Colorado State University. I guess he thought he'd stop on the way and—"

"I sent Chuck in with Baby Doe." Jack opened up the back door, disappeared inside for a moment.

A horse's hindquarters appeared at the door, the horse backing slowly down a ramp.

"Buckwheat!" Emily squealed. "You bringed my horsie!"

"Well, of course I brought your horsie!" Jack frowned, tying the reins to a hitch on the trailer's side. "When a little girl has a bad night like you had tonight, sometimes she just needs her horsie."

Megan was afraid she was going to cry again. She handed Emily to Jack, who carried her over to the gelding.

Buckwheat tossed his head and snorted a greeting.

Emily leaned forward, hugged the horse's neck. "Oh, Buckwheat, I'm so happy to see you. There was bad, bad man, and he was going to hurt Mommy, but Nate shot him, and he's gone now. I was so scared."

Buckwheat whickered, seeming to listen, tolerating Emily's affection with good spirits.

And then everyone crowded around, petting the horse's muzzle, patting his neck.

Megan's eyes filled with tears. "Thank you, Jack."

"You're welcome." His gaze was fixed on Emily, a suspicious sheen in his eyes. "And by the way, if I have a problem with you, you'll know it because I'll tell you. So don't you ever run out on me again, young lady. And know this—you've got a home at the ranch as long as you need one. Anyone who has a problem with that can get the hell off my payroll and off my land."

"Yes, sir." Megan felt Nate's arm go around her shoulder. She looked up at him. "Would you mind if Emily and I came home with you tonight?"

He kissed her forehead. "If you're sure it's what you want to do. I don't want to rush you. I want you to feel—"

She pressed a finger to his lips. "I'm sure."

In short order, Buckwheat was loaded back into the trailer and the doors secured.

Sophie appeared carrying one of her kids' car seats. "You can borrow it for as long as you need it. We have an extra."

"Thanks, Sophie." Megan gave her sister-in-law—and closest friend—a hug.

"Are you certain you want to do this?" Marc asked, his gaze following Nate, who was loading the car seat into the backseat of his truck.

"Yes, I am. I really care about him, Marc, and he cares about me."

"Alright then." Marc nodded. "Call if you need me."

"I will." Megan watched her brother walk away, Julian and Sophie beside him.

And as she stood there in the dark, something Nate had said last night came back to her.

It's not so much that the world won't forgive you, Megan, honey. It seems to me that you won't forgive yourself.

And she realized he was right. She'd never really forgiven herself—for what she'd done to her brother, for what she'd done to herself, for what she'd done to Emily.

But, how, exactly, did one forgive one's self?

Maybe she didn't have to figure that out tonight. Maybe it was enough just to know it was something she needed to do. Maybe it was enough for now just to be conscious of it.

And then Nate was there, beside her. "Are you ready?"

She nodded. "Yeah."

He wrapped his arm around her shoulder. "Let's get you home."

He walked her to his truck, opened the door for her, and steadied her as she climbed into the warmth of the cab. Emily was already sound asleep in the backseat, a blanket tucked around her. Then they set out, Jack following behind them with the horse trailer.

And as the lights of Denver disappeared in the rearview mirror, the mountains gleaming white in the moonlight ahead, Megan knew the weight of the past was still with her. But with Nate beside her, it no longer felt so heavy.

EPILOGUE

Seven months later

Alone for the first time all morning, Megan stared into the floor-length mirror.

A bride stared back at her.

If you had asked her last fall whether she'd be getting married in June, she would have laughed and shaken her head, knowing with one-hundred percent certainty that she would not. And yet here she was, about to marry a man she loved more than life, a man who cherished her, a man who had become a doting father to her precious daughter.

The bride in the mirror smiled.

The Vatana Watters gown had transformed her, lengths of ivory washed silk organza and silk taffeta making her feel like a princess, the intricately embroidered bodice fitting perfectly, the pink silk sash at her waist the perfect touch to make the gown a little less formal for an outdoor wedding. She wore nothing on her head, nothing on her wrists or throat, the princess-cut Canadian diamond studs Nate had given her for Christmas and her two-karat princess-cut engagement ring her only adornment. Her hair had been styled into waves, the sides drawn back into a silver barrette, the length of it left to spill over her shoulders. Her makeup was minimal. She looked... classy, beautiful, *happy*.

And she *was* happy—happier than she'd dreamed she could be.

She turned to the side, glanced down at the skirt and the chapel train, loving the way the dress moved, loving the way it made her feel.

What would Nate think?

He hadn't seen the gown. In fact, he hadn't seen her since yesterday morning at breakfast. She'd packed up and stayed at Marc's house for the night so that she and Sophie could focus on all the little details—manicure, pedicure, facial—and so that they could honor the tradition of the groom not seeing the bride before the wedding.

Nate had had his hands full anyway, getting the meadow at the picnic shelter ready for the wedding and two hundred guests. Though he hadn't wanted a bachelor party, Marc and Julian had insisted, getting all the guys together and dragging Nate through the bars of downtown Denver. Meanwhile, Sophie had invited her circle of friends over for a bachelorette party that had consisted of a dessert buffet, romantic comedies—and a few risqué gifts.

And now Megan was twenty minutes away from walking down the aisle.

A knock came at the door, and Sophie walked in, Emily behind her. Sophie was Megan's matron of honor and wore a Watters gown of soft blue, while Emily was the flower girl, her gown a tiny replica of Megan's, a crown of rosebuds on her blond head.

"Are you ready?" Sophie retrieved Megan's bouquet of pink cabbage roses. "The limo is here."

It was a ten-minute drive to the picnic shelter—the same route they'd traveled by sleigh last November.

Megan nodded, smiled. "Yes."

She felt like she'd waited a lifetime for this moment.

Another knock.

Sophie opened the door just a crack, then stepped back as Marc entered.

He took one look at Megan—and then just stared at her as if he'd never seen her before. "You look … *beautiful.*"

Megan smiled at his reaction. "Thanks. You look pretty decent yourself."

Dressed in a black summer tuxedo with an understated brown vest and brown and black striped silk tie, he looked much better than he had when he'd stumbled in the house drunk at three in the morning. He glanced over at Sophie. "Can I have just a minute with Megan?"

"Just don't make her cry. That's not waterproof mascara." Sophie reached for Emily's hand, still holding Megan's bouquet in the other. "We'll wait for you in the limo. Do you have to go potty, Emily?"

Marc waited until Sophie and Emily were gone, then drew Megan into his arms, and for a moment he just held her. "My baby sister is all grown up."

Megan fought the lump in her throat. "I wouldn't be standing here if it weren't for you. You know that, right? When I think of what I put you through… "

Marc had done so much for her, rescuing her from the streets, risking his life repeatedly, sacrificing six years of freedom to protect her.

He stepped back, tilted her head to meet his gaze. "Hey, you were never a burden. *Never.* Do you hear me?"

She nodded, felt the pricking of tears.

"Besides, you've got to give yourself some credit. *You* made yourself into the woman you are today. I am so damned proud you."

"I love you."

"I love you, too." He hugged her again, then drew back and looked at his watch. "We need to go. The groom is waiting."

N ate glanced at the time.
"Looking at your damned watch every ten seconds isn't going to make her get here any faster." The old man sat in the shade of the picnic shelter in his dress uniform, his medals polished, his Ranger tab as crisp and new as if he'd earned it last week and not fifty years ago. He grabbed another folding chair, opened it, motioned for Nate to sit.

Nate had no idea why he was nervous. It wasn't the stereotypical fear of tying the knot that men supposedly felt. He wasn't afraid to be married. He'd known a month into his relationship with Megan than he wanted her beside him for the rest of this life. If he could put a finger on what was making him so edgy it would be…

"I want everything to be perfect for her." Nate adjusted his saber and sat.

"It will be. Hell, son, that girl loves you so damned much you could ask her to marry you in a hog pen, and she'd say 'yes.'"

This made Nate grin in no small part because it was most likely true. "Were you nervous when you and Mom got married?"

His dad frowned as if struggling to recall. "I was a hell of a lot more hung over than you are, but, yeah, I guess I was."

At least the old man could admit it.

Nate took a deep breath, willed himself to enjoy the anticipation of watching Emily come down the aisle, of seeing Megan as a bride, of slipping the gold band his father carried in his jacket pocket onto her finger. "You do have the rings, right?"

His dad chuckled. "For the hundredth time, yes."

Paid staff bustled around, making sure everything was set up according to Nate and Megan's wishes. Guests milled about, some walking around the meadow, commenting on the view, others talking and laughing, some already seated. Old friends mingled with new, including the tight circle of friends Megan had inherited through her brother.

The men—most of them ex-military or law enforcement—had met through their wives, all of whom had worked for the Denver Independent's Investigative Team, or I-Team, at some point. Nate had gotten to know them all pretty well over the past several months. They were good people. He supposed he felt the strongest bond with McBride, who'd also served in special operations forces in Afghanistan—and earned a Medal of Honor for it. McBride lived pretty close by, and the two of them had knocked back more than a few beers sharing stories about friends they'd served with, both those who'd made it and those who'd died downrange.

It looked like everyone was already here *except* McBride. Still looking hung over, Darcangelo sat with his wife, Tessa, holding his six-month-old son, Tristan. Their daughter, Maire, who was a bit younger than Emily, bounded among the trees on imaginary horses with Hunter's son, Chase, and Reece and Kara's kids, Connor, Caitlyn and Brendan. Reece and Kara, meanwhile, were watching over Hunter and Sophie's little girl, Addison, who wanted to run and play with the others, but at the tender age of two couldn't quite keep up. Behind them sat Rossiter and his wife Kat with their little girl, Alissa, and baby boy, Nakai.

"Oh, McBride, it's just you." Nate heard Julian say. "I saw a flash of white and thought you were the bride."

"Head still hurting, Darcangelo? Drink less next time." A grin on his face, McBride appeared walking arm in arm with Natalie. He was wearing his Navy dress whites—complete with his Medal of Honor.

Nate and his father stood as McBride approached and saluted.

"Knock it off." McBride grinned, shaking their hands. "Congratulations. You're looking good. I always thought the Marines had the best dress uniform."

"Thanks." Nate grinned. "And, yes, we do."

"Thanks for joining us, McBride." Nate's dad said. "You honor us with the uniform. I don't think I've ever seen a Medal of Honor."

McBride ignored the praise, far too modest, in Nate's opinion, for a man who'd done so much for his country. "I'd like to introduce my wife, Natalie Benoit McBride. Natalie, this is Jack West, Nate's father. He served as an Army Ranger in Vietnam."

Natalie, a pretty brunette, smiled and shook the old man's hand, her New Orleans accent charming. "I've heard so much about you, Mr. West."

The old man chuckled. "Try not to hold it against me."

"Is there anything we can do to help?" Natalie asked.

"Nope," Jack shook his head. "You just make yourselves comfortable."

McBride leaned in, whispered in Nate's ear. "Relax. You'll do great."

Megan sat in the limousine holding her bouquet, Marc on one side of her and Sophie on the other, Emily sitting across from them with her little white basket of flower petals.

"You remember what you're supposed to do?" Sophie asked.

Emily nodded. "I walk toward Grandpa Jack and Daddy and throw my petals."

"That's right." Sophie shared a smile with Marc and Megan.

Megan looked out the window, watched the scenery pass. Perhaps it was her imagination or just her own joy that colored the afternoon, but the mountains seemed to be putting on an especially beautiful show today. The sky was cloudless and blindingly blue, the peaks still white with snow, green aspen leaves shivering in the breeze, columbines, purple penstemon, and golden banner scattering color across the forest floor.

This was her home. It would be her home for the rest of her life. Emily would grow up here on the Cimarron in the shadow of these mountains, together with any brothers or sisters that came along. Somehow knowing that gave Megan peace.

They were getting close, cars lining the road. And then, just ahead, she saw the white event tent that marked the south end of the meadow. Jack had rented it to serve both as a shelter for her in case of rain and to act as a kind of entrance to the meadow, preventing Nate from seeing her—and her from seeing Nate—until the wedding started.

"A bride needs to make a grand entrance," Jack had said. "Why the hell else spend that much money on a dress you're only going to wear once?"

And Megan felt a nervous flutter in her stomach.

The limo drew to a stop just behind the tent. Marc climbed out ahead of her, took her hand, and steadied her as she got out, while Sophie helped Emily. They walked into the tent together, the sound of chamber music drifting in from the other side. In the center of the tent, on a little table, Megan found a small velvet-covered box sitting beside an enormous bouquet of white roses, a card with her name on it propped up between them. She opened the card.

Here's a gift from an old man who's proud to welcome you officially to the family. Theresa would have adored you.

Love,

Jack

Megan opened the little box and gasped, fighting tears again.

Resting on velvet were Theresa West's mabe pearl earrings— the earrings she wore in the photograph on the fireplace mantel.

Emily bounced and hopped around the tent, but Megan was barely aware of her daughter's antics. Hands trembling, she removed her diamond studs, placed them carefully in the box, and put on the glowing pearls instead, slipping the box in Marc's tux pocket.

"The earrings belonged to Nate's mother," she explained to her brother, who peered over her shoulder at the card and then at her earlobes.

"Emily, honey, it's time to be quiet, okay?" Sophie said. "Listen for the harp so you'll know when it's your turn to go."

Megan tried to contain her emotions, taking slow, deep breaths while Marc and Sophie took turns peeking out the tent's front flap.

Sophie let out a little gasp. "Oh, look at Zach! I had no idea he was going to—"

And then music shifted, the harpist playing Pachelbel's Canon in D.

Megan bent down, gave her baby girl a kiss on the cheek. They'd come through so much, just the two of them. "Okay, Emily, sweet pea, it's time for you to walk down the aisle like we talked about."

Megan stepped back as Sophie opened the tent's door flap, a collective "aww" going up from their guests as Emily stepped out and started down the aisle.

Megan's gaze met Sophie's. "Thank you, Sophie. For everything. You're the greatest sister-in-law ever."

"Don't you dare make me cry." Sophie smiled, dabbing at teary eyes with a tissue. "I am so happy for you."

And then Sophie disappeared out the door, a bouquet of pink cabbage roses in her hands.

Marc offered Megan his arm, his gaze warm. "If you ever need me…"

She smiled. "I know."

Megan stepped out on Marc's arm, guests rising to their feet as she appeared.

The meadow had been transformed. It was bisected by a plush red runner, rows of chairs on either side forming an aisle, their backs garlanded with white organza, white ribbon, and bouquets of pink roses. Larger bouquets flanked the meadow sitting atop tall white stands that looked like Greek columns. The picnic shelter stood in the background and had been decorated like the chairs, with garlands of shimmering white organza, white ribbon, and pink roses.

But all Megan could see was Nate.

He stood at the end of the aisle beside Jack and Rev. Marshall wearing not a tux, but his Marine Corps dress uniform, the left side of his midnight blue jacket glittering with medals, a saber at his side, a white cap on his head.

He looked so stunningly handsome, so proud, that it made her heart ache.

And his gaze was riveted on her.

Nate had imagined this moment a dozen times over the past few weeks, but nothing he'd imagined could come close to the vision that was Megan. She walked slowly toward him, head high, sunlight striking sparks of copper off her hair, the breeze tugging at the filmy cloth of her slender skirts. Her gown was simple, understated, feminine, the neckline low enough to draw his gaze, the narrow waist emphasizing the soft curve of her hips.

She looked like an angel—his angel.

God, he loved her. He loved her more than he would ever be able to tell her, but at least he had the rest of his life to try.

He blinked, his vision suddenly blurry.

Tears?

"Breathe, son."

Nate drew in a deep breath, blinked, glanced down—and saw that the old man had tears in his eyes, too.

As Megan drew near, their gazes met and held, her green eyes glittering, her cheeks flushed, her lips curved in a soft smile.

Nate stepped forward, held out his hand. Hunter took hers, placed it in Nate's—and then just stood there.

"Marc?" she whispered.

"Yeah?"

"Let go."

"Right."

Nate met Hunter's gaze, gave him a nod, a silent understanding passing between them.

You'd better damned well take care of my little sister.

You damned well know I will.

Then Rev. Marshall began to speak. "We are gathered in this beautiful place to celebrate the joining of this man and this woman in matrimony."

Nate knew he should be paying attention, but he couldn't seem to wrap his mind around anything beyond the woman beside him— the glow of her skin, her scent, the warm feel of her hand in his. Somehow he managed to say his vows, slip a gold band on her finger, help her slide a gold band onto his, the rest of the world seeming distant, time frozen as he looked into her eyes. "I love you."

"I love *you*."

And then he was kissing her—or she was kissing him—soft lips caressing, the scent of her skin filling his lungs, the taste of her on his tongue. He drew her closer, needing to hold her, needing to feel her against him.

"What God has joined so perfectly and miraculously, let no one put asunder." From somewhere far away, Nate heard Rev. Marshall's voice. "I was going to say, 'You may kiss the bride,' but they beat me to it."

Laughter.

"Lord have mercy!" The reverend was chuckling. "By the authority vested in me by the state of Colorado, I pronounce you husband and wife."

Cheers. Applause. Whistles.

Little arms around Nate's legs.

He looked down, saw Emily, crowned with roses, smiling up at them, a living ray of sunshine. He bent down, scooped her up, kissed his little girl on the cheek.

"Now you're my real daddy!"

"You bet I am." Nate met Megan's gaze.

And in her eyes, he saw forever.

Keep Reading for an exclusive I-Team Short, *Marc and Julian Make a Beer Run.*

MARC AND JULIAN MAKE A BEER RUN

An I-Team Short
By Pamela Clare

Dedicated to the members of the I-Team Facebook group

Marc Hunter kicked back on Zach McBride's deck, letting his bare chest soak up the rays and sipping a cold Fat Tire. The newlyweds—Megan, Marc's younger sister, and her husband, Nate West—had just gotten back from their honeymoon in Scotland, and Zach and his wife Natalie had invited the gang over for a barbeque to welcome them home. Food, beer, a day in the mountains—what was there not to love about that?

Inside the McBride house, the women were looking at Megan's photos from Scotland and watching over the smaller children. Down on the lawn, West, Gabe Rossiter, Reece Sheridan, and Joaquin Ramirez tossed a pigskin back and forth with the older kids. But here on the deck was where Marc wanted to be—sunshine, beer, and the scent of sizzling beef.

"Okay, here it is."

Marc opened his eyes to see Julian Darcangelo step outside carrying his new baby, ready to show it off for the first time. Darcangelo set the black case down on the patio table and opened it, giving Marc just a glimpse before West, Rossiter, Sheridan, and Ramirez, who'd ditched the pigskin, blocked his view.

"Hey, guys, I can't see a damned thing with you in the way." Marc gave an impatient kick.

The guys ignored him, "oohing" and "aahing" over Darcangelo's latest acquisition.

"Try getting off your ass." McBride offered with a grin, flipping burgers on his new fancy-ass built-in gas grill (which, Marc suspected, was the *real* reason they'd all been invited over).

Marc glared at him, got to his feet, and peered over West's shoulder at a brand spanking new SIG Sauer P239 Tactical pistol. As a former Army Special Forces sniper who now worked as a marksman for Denver SWAT, Marc's gun lust was reserved mostly for rifles and optics, though he always carried a concealed 9mm for personal protection. "Nice."

They all watched while Darcangelo took it out, locked the slide open, checked to make sure the weapon was clear, then aimed it out toward the forest.

"Why'd you decide to go with this instead of something like the Bodyguard?" Ramirez asked. "This is for off-duty concealed carry, right?"

Ramirez had taken an interest in firearms ever since he'd survived that attack on the tour bus in Mexico. He'd made more than a few trips to the gun range with Marc and the guys, and was a deadly shot with his Glock 22.

"The threaded barrel is one thing." Darcangelo held the new pistol flat on his outstretched palm. "I can attach a suppressor if I want to take this into action on-duty. Also, the magazine carries eight rounds. The magazine on the Bodyguard only loads six. But I guess the big thing for me was the feel and the caliber. The Bodyguard is a small weapon, and I have big hands. And I feel better about firing nine millimeter than I do three-eighty ACP."

Darcangelo handed the weapon to Ramirez, who was a photojournalist by profession.

"God, this is sweet." Ramirez released the slide lock, then sighted on the forest, before passing it over to Sheridan.

"Got a case of gun envy, Ramirez?" McBride asked.

"You know it."

"A three-eighty round will put someone down, won't it?" Sheridan also sighted, before popping the magazine out and sliding it back in.

"Sure it will—most of the time." Marc took the pistol from Sheridan, tested its weight in his hand, sighted, then passed the SIG on to West. "Sometimes you get a guy who's hopped up on cocaine or meth or is just plain psycho, and he won't even feel a smaller round. You want to stop someone? Go with nine millimeter—or, better yet, forty-five."

"What do you carry, Nate?" Sheridan, who'd just resigned his position as a high school teacher to make a run for lieutenant governor, was no slouch when it came to pistol marksmanship, even if he didn't have the military or law enforcement experience that most of them had.

"A Colt M1911." West, a former Marine special operator, passed the P239 over to Rossiter. "It's slender enough to carry concealed. I can carry it cocked and locked, and it fires a forty-five round. I don't care what anyone says about nine millimeter—"

"Oh, here he goes again." Darcangelo rolled his eyes.

"—there's a reason they say, 'They all fall to ball.' Besides, I don't need a rail and all that fancy shit. I just want a reliable weapon that fires a powerful round."

"Spoken like a true jarhead, West." Darcangelo shook his head.

"I'm fine with nine millimeter." Rossiter was a former Mountain Parks Ranger and paramedic who now test-drove prosthetic legs for extreme athletes. "I've got a Glock 26 for concealed carry and an HK forty-caliber semi-auto for home defense."

His stomach growling, Marc walked over to look at the burgers, but McBride shoed him away. "I figured you just had some sort of James Bond rig in your fake leg—flex your ankle and fifty-cal rounds shoot out of your heel or some shit."

"Who says I don't?" Rossiter handed the weapon back to Darcangelo.

"How about you, McBride?" Sheridan asked.

"On duty, I pack a pair of Springfield TRP pistols." McBride, a former Navy SEAL, was the chief deputy U.S. Marshal for the Colorado territory and the second highest ranking law enforcement officer in the state.

"They fire forty-five, in case you're wondering, Darcangelo," West added with a grin, rubbing the point in.

McBride went on. "If I want to conceal off duty, I've got a few to choose from—a SIG P239, a Bodyguard, a Walther PPS, a Ruger..."

The door opened, and Natalie walked out with an empty platter.

"Gun talk. I should've known." She rose up on her tiptoes and kissed her husband's cheek. "Zach shops for guns the way many women shop for shoes and purses—it's constant and ongoing."

This made the guys chuckle.

Natalie held out the empty platter. "I hope those burgers are done. The kids are starving. Apparently, their parents never allow them to eat except when they come to our house—and then they eat everything."

"Perfect timing." McBride lifted the burgers one at a time off the grill and put them on the plate. "I'll get our steaks going. If I acknowledged the appearance of sexism in this request and promised to make up for it by doing something that honors your equality, would you mind grabbing me another beer?"

Natalie smiled, but shook her head. "I think Marc took the last one."

Six heads turned Marc's way.

"Nice." Ramirez looked pissed.

Darcangelo glared at him. "Way to go, Hunter."

"Hey, this was my first and only." Marc pointed to the bottle in his right hand.

But McBride was still staring at Natalie. "Are you saying we're out of beer?"

Natalie carried the full platter toward the door, which Darcangelo opened for her. "Didn't you make it to the liquor store? We've got some wine coolers and a bottle of chardonnay already chilled."

Wine coolers? Chardon-fucking-ay?

The guys exchanged glances.

And Marc knew what he had to do. He tossed back the rest of his Fat Tire, sat the empty bottle down, and reached for his shirt. "No problem. I'll head into Evergreen on a beer run."

Darcangelo snapped his gun case shut, locked it. "I'll go with you."

How Marc's volunteering to make a beer run with Darcangelo had turned into six men packed into McBride's SUV— Ramirez had been called out on assignment—Marc couldn't say. The moment the women had heard they were going into town, they'd been pelted with requests. Kat James, Rossiter's wife, needed baby wipes. Kara McMillan, Reece's wife, had forgotten to bring ice cream to put on top the pie. And Megan wanted something of a personal and private nature, which she had revealed only to her husband.

And their beer strike force had become an expedition.

"Here's how we'll do this." Marc looked back over his shoulder. "Alpha Team—that's me, Darcangelo, and McBride—will take the liquor store, dropping off Beta Team—that's Sheridan, Rossiter, and you, West—"

"Whoa! Wait a minute!" Rossiter cut Marc off. "I'm not part of any *beta* team."

"Yeah, me neither," West added. "And don't even suggest 'Baby Wipe Patrol' or 'Tampon Squadron.'"

So that's what Megan had wanted.

"Okay, fine." Marc nodded. "Alpha Team will take the liquor store, dropping Team One off at the grocery store. We rendezvous at the vehicle in the liquor store parking lot at eighteen-hundred hours."

They had their strategy. Each man knew what he had to do.

Marc would be back relaxing on the deck in no time.

Marc followed Darcangelo and McBride through the door of the liquor store, a bell jingling as they entered. The place was all but empty, Led Zeppelin's *Dyer Maker* playing on the sound system, the air conditioning blasting. A pretty young woman stood behind the counter. A kid with tattoos, saggy pants, and metal bits in his face was the only other customer.

"Where are your refrigerated microbrews?" Darcangelo called out.

The young woman—early twenties, five-five, blond—said nothing, but pointed toward a refrigeration unit against the rear wall, watching them as they moved through the store. Marc might not have given her a second look had their gazes not collided in that moment. In her eyes, he saw terror.

Everything seemed to slow down as he took it all in. The woman's dilated pupils and rapid breathing. The kid with the tattoos seemingly perusing French wines—*yeah, right*—his gaze furtively following Marc and the guys. The slightly open cash drawer.

They'd arrived in time to interrupt a robbery.

"Rossiter wants us to pick up a six-pack of Boulder Beer's Never Summer Ale if they have it and Sweaty Betty if they don't," Darcangelo was saying. "Twisted Pine brews an Oak Whiskey Red that is fan-freaking-tastic."

"Fat Tire is good enough for me," McBride said. "I had some chili beer down in Mexico that was the best damned brew I've ever had with steak, but I know I'm not going to find that here."

Marc needed to get their attention. He stopped, turned as if he were heading off to the wine section. "I think I'm going to grab that bottle of chardonnay Natalie wanted. Got to keep my wife happy."

They stopped and looked back at him, their law enforcement instincts catching up with their facial expressions by the time his words sank in.

"Sounds good." Darcangelo's gaze moved quickly from the woman at the counter to the man with the tattoos.

"Get something from California. I hear French wines suck this time of year." McBride glanced covertly at the dome mirror on the ceiling.

There on its distorted round surface, Marc saw a second man crouched down behind the counter next to the cashier. And the bastard was armed.

While Darcangelo and McBride kept up the beer chatter, each of them picking up a couple of six packs, Marc walked over to the wine section. "Got any California chardonnays on sale?"

The woman at the register was growing more and more afraid, her gaze darting nervously from Marc to the man with the tattoos, her face pale. "N-no."

Marc stopped at an endcap display of white wines and pretended to read the labels, trying to keep one eye on the woman and the other on the kid with the tattoos, waiting for Darcangelo and McBride to get into position. "You know, I have no clue what the difference is between a Riesling, a Pinot Grigio, and chardonnay. They're all white, right?"

The woman at the counter gave a wooden nod, clearly very close to panic. But Darcangelo and McBride were on their way to the counter now.

She didn't know it, but she was about to be saved.

"You think this is enough for all of us?" Darcangelo asked, setting two six packs down on the counter and pulling out his wallet.

"I don't know." McBride set his beer down on the counter, too—Rossiter's Sweaty Betty and some IPA. "How much are you planning on drinking? Didn't you learn your lesson at West's bachelor party?"

"You've got a point." Darcangelo turned toward the woman. "I'll just take these today together with …" In the blink of an eye, he reached behind the counter, grabbed the gunman by his hair and jerked him to his feet, dragging him across the counter and pinning him there. "… *this* piece of shit."

The gunman yelped, something heavy clattering to the ground— a Glock 19.

The tattooed kid reached for a weapon concealed inside his jacket, but Marc had already drawn, his Taurus PT 709 aimed at the idiot's chest. "Don't even think about it. Down on the ground! *Now!*"

Tattoo Kid slowly got to his knees, a sneer on his acne-scarred face.

"What's your name? Christy? It's going to be all right now, Christy," Darcangelo said to the terrified cashier, his tone of voice shifting from soothing to mocking as he spoke to the assailant. "You like to carry guns and scare women? You're in deep shit, asshole."

"Fuck you, you fucking pussy!"

The cashier was weeping softly, near to hysterics. "M-my dad…"

Marc heard McBride dialing 911 over the rasping sound of duct tape being torn from a roll.

"This is McBride. I want to report an armed robbery at Evergreen Liquor. Three off-duty law enforcement officers are on the scene. Requesting backup."

Tattoo Kid's sneer disappeared. "You're cops?"

"Not your day, is it?" Marc moved in, weapon aimed, finger on the trigger.

"No, man, it's not *your* day."

Marc ignored the kid's bravado. "Lie flat on your stomach, legs spread, hands behind your head. Oh, look, you're a pro. I bet you've done this before."

He patted the guy down, found a Cobra 9 mm in his jacket and a switchblade in his front jeans pocket. "I've always wanted to ask this question. Why do you walk around with sagging pants? Do you think it's sexy? Does it make you look tough? 'Look how bad I am. I don't even pull up my pants.' You look stupid, man. Chicks don't like it. I bet you never get laid or even—"

Rat-at-at-at-at-at-at!

A scream. Shattered glass. Spraying liquid. The scent of alcohol.

High-caliber rounds poured out of nowhere, blasting bottles to bits, turning the floor into a slick mess of liquor and broken glass.

Marc dove for the floor, shards and slivers cutting his skin, alcohol stinging the cuts as he scrambled on his forearms toward the kid, who tried to get to his feet, clearly hoping to run.

"Bad fucking idea!" Marc shouted, pressing the barrel of his Taurus against the son of a bitch's cheek.

So that's what the kid had meant about it not being their day. Somewhere in the store was a third assailant—one who wasn't afraid to shoot at cops.

Then the lights went out.

From across the store came McBride's voice.

"Okay. This shit just got real."

Knowing he needed to neutralize the kid so he could deal with the shooter, Marc turned his pistol in his hand and struck him upside the temple, knocking him out. Keeping low, Marc made his way toward the center aisle.

"You fucking pigs, listen to me!" The voice came from the back of the store. "Put down your guns, and let Trance and Havoc go! I've got the girl's dad back here, and I'll shoot him in the fucking face if you fuck with us!"

The woman was crying.

Great. Just what we need—a hostage situation.

McBride answered. "We've already called for police backup. There's no way out of this now except for you to put down your weapon and let the man go. You've already shot one of my partners and killed one of your friends. Don't make this harder on yourself."

Marc glanced around the endcap, made eye contact with McBride, who crouched on this side of the counter next to the assailant he and Darcangelo had brought down. The man lay on his belly on the floor, mad as hell, his wrists and ankles bound with duct tape, his mouth covered.

So McBride was bluffing.

But where was Darcangelo? He must have taken cover behind the counter with the woman, trying to protect her.

McBride signaled to Marc.

One shooter. Ten o'clock.

Marc nodded

He worked his way silently back the way he'd come, stepping carefully over the unconscious form of Tattoo Kid, his shoes grinding slivers of glass into the floor, the reek of alcohol overpowering.

"Who's dead?" Panic slid into the shooter's voice. "Trance? Havoc?"

"The ugly one with the tattoos," McBride answered.

"Trance! Oh, God!" The shooter sounded so young, just a kid.

"I tell you what. We'll cut you a deal." McBride was trying to distract the shooter, buying time for Marc to find him and take him out. "You send the man out to us and run out the back door, and we won't follow you."

"Fuck you! You think I'm stupid?"

"I think you're in big trouble if you don't wise up right away."

Only half-hearing the conversation, Marc made his way aisle by shattered aisle toward the back, searching the store for any sign of the shooter. He didn't want to get too close. If the shooter's weapon was outfitted with optics, he'd see Marc before Marc saw him, and then this beer run would turn into a last op.

Near the back of the store, he stopped, got down, and watched for any sign of movement. And there, inside the refrigeration unit, he saw the dark outline of a man, legs visible between shelves, the barrel of a what looked like an AK knock-off jutting out from between broken champagne bottles.

But how was Marc going to reach him? Getting inside the refrigeration unit—Marc could see now that it was actually a big walk-in refrigerator with shelf units that faced into the store—would mean exposing himself. He couldn't fire on the guy because he had no idea where the hostage was.

"Is a few hundred bucks worth life in prison?" McBride asked.

Marc could answer that question.

No. Fucking. Way.

"You got kids? A mom who loves you? Anyone you care about? If you don't send the girl's father out right now, you're not going to see them again."

"Shut the fuck up! Shit! Shit!" The shooter was starting to break.

Movement.

Marc's gaze shifted to the opposite side of the room.

Darcangelo.

Marc pointed toward the door with a jerk of his head, saw Darcangelo nod, then disappear.

A moment later, a single bottle tipped onto the floor and rolled down the far aisle, the sound drawing the panicked shooter's attention, the barrel of his rifle now pointing away from Marc.

In a blink, Marc was on his feet. Keeping low, he slipped as silently as he could through the door that led to the back rooms of the store. He slowly made his way along a concrete wall and around stacks of cardboard boxes to the refrigerator's entrance. The door stood ajar.

He took a breath, mentally preparing himself, then pivoted, aiming his weapon at the shooter, his body partially shielded by the thick steel door. "Drop your weapon! Drop it! Now!"

The AK fell to the floor with a clatter, and Marc found himself looking into the eyes of a panicked boy who couldn't have been a day over eighteen, if that.

He lunged for his weapon, but Marc kicked it to the side. "Oh, no you don't! Freeze!"

But the kid was desperate.

He ran at Marc, aiming a high kick at his head.

Marc ducked, holstered his weapon. "You want to play? Have it your way."

But then Darcangelo was behind him. "I've got this, Hunter. You go find the girl's dad. I'll handle Karate Kid, here. I haven't had a good workout in weeks."

Marc gave Darcangelo a nod and headed off down the hallway, the sound of sparring following him as he went—a thud, a groan, and Darcangelo's voice.

"You threw yourself off balance there. You're angry and afraid, and it's fucking with your concentration. Try again."

At the end of the hallway on the left, Marc found a man who looked to be in his fifties tied up with an extension cord, a sock shoved in his mouth. Pale and covered with sweat, he looked at Marc with wide, pleading eyes, and Marc knew exactly what the poor guy wanted to know. "I'm Marc Hunter, Denver SWAT. Christy's safe. Everything's going to be okay."

Marc pulled the sock from his mouth and untied him, the open safe on the wall and the backpack on the floor telling him what had been happening back here when they'd walked in.

"Thank God! Thank God you came!" The man got unsteadily to his feet.

Marc rested a hand on his shoulder. "You okay?"

"Yeah. I will be. Did they hurt my girl?"

"I don't think so. Let's get you out of here."

When they reached the refrigerator, Darcangelo was binding the shooter's wrists with duct tape, the kid bleeding from his nose and a cut on his lip. "You've got some skills, but you're not using them for any good purpose. You really fucked up today, and you're going to pay for it. But the way I see it, this is a chance to rethink your life, straighten your head out."

The big guy had kicked the kid's ass—and then gone Zen master on him.

Marc stuck his head in. "You done fucking around, Dickangelo?"

"Yeah, just about."

Out front, McBride was opening a bottle of water for Christy, who leapt to her feet and ran into her father's embrace. "Oh, Daddy!"

Then Marc heard a groan and caught a glimpse of Trance—if that really was the kid's name—staggering out the front door, a hand pressed against his temple.

"Shit." Hunter started after him, certain the kid wouldn't make it far, police sirens wailing in the distance.

Then the door opened again, the bell jingling.

West stepped cautiously inside, weapon drawn.

"Sorry, West, but you guys missed all the action."

"Nope. Not all of it." He opened the door once more, stepping aside to make room for Rossiter and Sheridan, who were supporting Trance's weight between them, the kid's face screwed up with pain, his skin pale, beads of sweat on his forehead.

"What happened to him?" Marc hadn't hit him that hard.

Sheridan grinned. "West told him to stop, and when the kid refused, Gabe tried to trip him, but ended up kicking him in the balls."

Marc winced. *Ouch!* "With which foot?"

Rossiter shrugged. "The titanium alloy one."

Every man in the liquor store groaned.

An hour later, the guys pulled into McBride's driveway, the SUV reeking of alcohol from the liquor in Marc's clothes, the back loaded with enough microbrew beer, scotch, wine, and champagne for an entire summer's worth of barbecues—gifts from the liquor shop's grateful owner. The women were waiting for them when they drove up, McBride having called Natalie to tell her what had happened.

Marc's gaze sought and found Sophie, who stood just outside the front door holding little Addy. They'd been married five years now, but every time he looked at her, he felt the same hitch in his chest he'd felt that first night they'd had sex under the stars back in high school. "Hey, hon."

Her eyes went wide when she saw the cuts and blood on his arms. She hurried toward him. "You're hurt! Ew! You smell like a distillery."

Marc chuckled, kissed her on the cheek. "One of the kids opened fire, and I ended up crawling through glass shards and a puddle of booze."

"Thank God no one was hurt!"

"You can shower upstairs, Hunter." McBride walked past him carrying a case of Fat Tire. "I'll loan you some jeans and a T-shirt."

"Thanks."

A half an hour later, Marc was back in his seat on the deck, a tumbler of fifty-year-old Macallan in his hand, the sun setting over the Rockies, the scent of grilling steaks making his mouth water. Sophie sat beside him sipping champagne, her fingers laced through his, the kids all downstairs watching *Up*.

While the steaks grilled, the guys filled in the details, telling the women exactly what had happened.

"So then I walk back out with the shop owner, and Darcangelo is trussing the kid up and playing sensei, offering him advice. 'Find purpose for your life, Grasshopper.'"

"Maybe some of it will get through to him."

Marc gave a snort. "The kid threatened to kill three law enforcement officers then tried to fight me when I was pointing a gun straight at him. I don't see a lot of hope there for reform."

Darcangelo shrugged. "When I was his age, I had already killed a man."

Tessa got to her feet, walked tipsily over to her husband. "Such cheerful conversation. Do you think other people talk about robberies, shootings, and murder over dinner? I'm hungry."

Everyone laughed.

Kat shifted her sleeping baby boy from one arm to the other, her gaze on her husband. "Did you mean to kick that kid *there*?"

Rossiter looked sheepish. "Well... Not really."

West glared at him. "The hell you didn't. You broke the Man Code, dude. 'No man shall knowingly and with malice aforethought kick another man in the nuts.'"

"Okay, so I kicked him in the nuts. The little fucker was fleeing the scene of a crime where he'd pointed a weapon at my buddies."

Kat said something in Navajo that made Rossiter grin.

"Here's the thing I don't understand." Kara got to her feet and walked toward the patio table to refill her wine glass. "You men just had an experience that most of us would consider to be a nightmare, and you *enjoyed* it. I'd like to think the humor is just your way of dealing with the tension of having been in a life-threatening situation, but I think you actually *enjoyed* it."

McBride grinned. "You know what they say—do what you love."

Natalie rolled her eyes. "You *love* getting shot at?"

Megan looked accusingly at West. "You're all adrenaline junkies."

"Me?" West looked defensively back at her. "Hey, I was in the store buying you, er … something … when this happened, remember?"

That made everyone laugh again.

Marc had his own perspective. "The way I see it, we made a difference in the lives of that liquor store owner and his daughter today. Who knows what would have happened to them if we hadn't shown up when we did. We weren't on duty, but we did our job, and we did it well. Because of that, three criminals are behind bars, and those two are safe tonight. When it works out like it did this afternoon, I *do* enjoy it. It's one hell of a feeling to go to bed at night knowing you got someone dangerous off the streets or saved someone's life."

Natalie raised her glass, looking from one woman to the next. "To our husbands and all the brave men and women like them."

"Hear, hear!"

"Cheers!"

Glasses and bottles were raised, Marc meeting each man's gaze before sipping, the scotch burning a sweet path to his stomach.

Sophie looked up at him, her gaze soft. "That was beautiful."

He kissed her cheek, the scotch and her scent warming his blood. "Thanks."

Oh, yeah. He was *so* getting laid tonight.

OTHER TITLES BY PAMELA CLARE

I-Team Series (in order)

Extreme Exposure (Book 1)

Heaven Can't Wait (Book 1.5)

Hard Evidence (Book 2)

Unlawful Contact (Book 3)

Naked Edge (Book 4)

Breaking Point (Book 5)

Skin Deep: An I-Team After Hours novella (Book 5.5)

Kenleigh/Blakewell Family Saga

Sweet Release (Book 1)

Carnal Gift (Book 2)

Ride the Fire (Book 3) — Coming February 5, 2013.

MacKinnon's Rangers series

Surrender (Book 1)

Untamed (Book 2)

Defiant (Book3)

ABOUT THE AUTHOR

Colorado author Pamela Clare began her writing career as a columnist and investigative reporter and eventually became the first woman editor-in-chief of two different newspapers. Along the way, she and her team won numerous state and national honors, including the National Journalism Award for Public Service. In 2011, Clare was awarded the Keeper of the Flame Lifetime Achievement Award for her body of work. A single mother with two sons, she writes historical romance and contemporary romantic suspense at the foot of the beautiful Rocky Mountains. Visit her website at www.pamelaclare.com.

Twitter: @Pamela_Clare

Rock*It Reads: www.rockitreads.com

Check out Pamela Clare and the I-Team Group on Facebook.

21466122R00118

Made in the USA
Lexington, KY
15 March 2013